"Mr. van der Bee[k] what he's given or go hungry."

Patience, who was examining the diminished contents of the kitchen cupboard, hadn't realized she'd spoken out loud—or that she was no longer alone.

"He'll eat it. Don't worry," said Mr. van der Beek, smiling as she jumped at the sound of his voice.

"How long have you been standing there?" she demanded, turning to face him.

"I was admiring your legs—they're very attractive, Patience."

She gave him a steady look.

"Do you always blush when you are paid a compliment?" he wanted to know blandly.

"I don't know." Despite her red cheeks, Patience spoke matter-of-factly. "I can't remember ever being paid one."

Betty Neels is well-known for her romances set in the Netherlands, which is hardly surprising. She married a Dutchman and spent the first twelve years of their marriage living in Holland and working as a nurse. Today, she and her husband make their home in an ancient stone cottage in England's West Country, but they return to Holland often. She loves to explore tiny villages and tour privately owned homes there in order to lend an air of authenticity to the background of her books.

Books by Betty Neels

AN OLD-FASHIONED GIRL

GIRL

Betty Neels

Harlequin Books

TORONTO • NEW YORK • LONDON
AMSTERDAM • PARIS • SYDNEY • HAMBURG
STOCKHOLM • ATHENS • TOKYO • MILAN
MADRID • WARSAW • BUDAPEST • AUCKLAND

ISBN 0-373-03287-0

AN OLD-FASHIONED GIRL

Copyright © 1992 by Betty Neels.

This edition published by arrangement with Harlequin Enterprises B. V.

® and TM are trademarks of the publisher. Trademarks indicated with
® are registered in the United States Patent and Trademark Office, the
Canadian Trade Marks Office and in other countries.

Printed in U.S.A.

CHAPTER ONE

THE two men stood at the window, contemplating the dreary January afternoon outside, and then by common consent turned to look at the room in which they were.

'Of course,' observed the elder of the two, a short, stout man with a thatch of grey hair and a craggy face, 'Norfolk—this part of rural Norfolk—during the winter months is hardly welcoming.' Despite his words he sounded hopefully questioning.

'I do not require a welcome.' His companion's deep voice had the trace of an accent. 'I require peace and quiet.' He glanced around him at the pleasant, rather shabby room, apparently impervious to the chill consequence to the house's having lain empty for some weeks. 'Today is the sixth—I should like to come in four days' time. I shall have my housekeeper with me, but perhaps you can advise me as to the best means of getting help for the house.'

'That should be no difficulty, Mr van der Beek. There are several women in the village only too willing to oblige and should you require someone to keep the garden in order there is old Ned Groom who was the gardener here...'

'Excellent.' Mr van der Beek turned to look out of the window again. He was an extremely tall man, heavily built and still in his thirties, with a commanding nose in a handsome face, a firm mouth and light clear blue eyes. His hair was so fair that it was difficult to see where it was already silvered with grey. 'I will take the house for six months—perhaps you would undertake the paperwork.'

'Of course.' The older man hesitated. 'You mentioned that you required peace and quiet above all else. Might I suggest that you should employ someone: a general factotum, as it were, to relieve you of the tiresome interruptions which are bound to occur—the telephone, the tradespeople, bills to be paid, the tactful handling of unwelcome visitors, the care of your house should you wish to go away for a few days...'

'A paragon, in fact.' Mr van der Beek's voice was dry.

His companion chose to take him literally. 'Indeed, yes. A local person well known in the village and therefore someone who would not be resented and is the soul of discretion. Your housekeeper need have no fear that her authority will be undermined.'

Mr van der Beek took his time to consider that. 'It is probably a good idea, but it must be made clear to this person that she—it is a she, I presume?—will come on a month's trial. I will leave you to make that clear and also to deal with the wages and so forth.'

'What wages had you in mind?'

Mr van der Beek waved a large impatient hand. 'My dear fellow, I leave that to your discretion.' He went to the door. 'Can I give you a lift back to Aylsham?'

His companion accepted eagerly and they left together, locking the door carefully behind them before getting into the dark blue Bentley parked in the drive before the house. Aylsham was something under twenty miles away and they had little to say to each other but, as Mr van der Beek drew up before the estate agent's office in the main street, he asked,

'You have my solicitor's number? Presumably the owner of the house has a solicitor of her own?'

'Of course. I shall contact them immediately. Rest assured that the house will be ready for you when you return in four days' time.'

They bade each other goodbye and Mr van der Beek drove himself on to Norwich and on down the A140 before cutting across country to Sudbury and Saffron Walden, and, still keeping to the smaller roads, to London. It would have been quicker to have taken the A11 but he had time to spare and he wanted to go over his plans. It had taken careful planning to arrange for six months away from his work as a consultant surgeon; his meticulous notes had reached the stage when they could be transformed into a textbook on surgery and he had spent some weeks searching for a suitable place in which to live while he wrote it. He was fairly sure that he had found it—at least, he profoundly hoped so.

The house agent watched him go and then hurried into his office and picked up the phone, dialled a number and waited impatiently for someone to answer. He didn't give the dry-as-dust voice time to say more than his name. 'George? Dr van der Beek has taken the Martins' house for six months. He wants to move in in four days' time. I'm to engage daily help and when I suggested he might need someone to help the housekeeper he's bringing with him he agreed. Will you see Patience as soon as possible? I didn't tell him that she was the niece of the owners, but in any case I don't think he will notice her; he wants complete quiet while he writes a book. Provided she can keep out of sight and get along with the housekeeper the job's hers...'

Mr George Bennett coughed. 'It is very short notice—the paperwork...'

'Yes, yes, I know, but the Martins need the money very badly, and besides, Patience can add something to that miserable pension of theirs. It's a godsend.'

Mr Bennett coughed again. 'I will go and see Patience this afternoon. It is getting a little late; however I do agree with you that this is a chance not to be missed. Was the question of salary raised?'

'No, but he drives a Bentley and didn't quibble over the rent. I think it might be a good idea if she were to call and see the housekeeper—she's coming with Mr van der Beek. I rather fancy that he will leave the running of the house to her.'

'Very well. I shall go and see Patience now and make sure that everything is in order by the tenth. Shall we leave it to her to engage the help needed?'

'I should think so. She is well known here and liked. There should be no difficulty.'

Patience Martin, standing at her bedroom window with a pile of freshly ironed linen in her arms, watched Mr Bennett coming along the street, his elderly person sheltering under an umbrella. The street was narrow and quiet, lined with small flat-fronted houses, all exactly alike, and he was obviously making for her aunts' front door. She put down the linen and ran downstairs in time to prevent him thumping the knocker; her aunts were dozing before their tea and they were too old and frail to be wakened to listen to bad news. For that was what it would be, she reflected; ever since they had lost almost all their capital in a company which had gone bankrupt her aunts regarded old Mr Bennett as the harbinger of bad news...it was he who had warned them that they would have to leave their home—sell it or rent it and live on the proceeds, and that frugally. Having lived in moderate comfort for all their lives they had been quite bewildered but uncomplaining, moving to the poky little house he had found for them, quite unable to appreciate the situation. It was Patience who had coped with the difficulties, paid bills and shopped with an economical eye, contriving to give them their glass of sherry before lunch and Earl Grey tea, extravagances offset by the cheaper cuts of meat skilfully disguised and cod instead of halibut...

She reached the door in time to open it before Mr Bennett could knock, and she ushered him inside. In the narrow hall she took his umbrella, helped him off with his coat, informed him in her quiet voice that her aunts were asleep and ushered him into the sitting-room. It was a small room, overfurnished with her aunts' most treasured pieces but cheaply carpeted and curtained. Mr Bennett took an outsize armchair upholstered in worn brocade and put his briefcase down beside it.

'If it's bad news perhaps you'll tell me first,' suggested Patience in a matter-of-fact voice.

Mr Bennett, not to be hurried, studied her as she sat down opposite him. A pity that she was possessed of such unassuming features, he thought; lovely grey eyes fringed with black lashes, long and thick, were the only asset in her face with its too short nose, wide mouth and hair brushed firmly back into a careless bun. Very abundant hair, and silky, but most definitely mouse.

'My dear Patience, for once I bring good news. Your aunts' house has been let at a very good rent for six months, payable monthly in advance, which should allow you to live without worries for the time being.'

Patience, thinking of the small pile of bills waiting to be settled, sighed with relief. 'When does the new tenant come?'

'In four days' time. A Mr van der Beek, a surgeon who needs time to write a book of reference. He emphasises that he must have complete quiet while he is working and has chosen your aunts' house for that reason. He is bringing his housekeeper with him but he has asked Mr Tomkins to find help in the village for the household and, since he was so emphatic about being left undisturbed while he writes, Mr Tomkins suggested that he might like to employ someone to act as a buffer between him and any hindrances—the telephone, tradespeople, unwelcome callers and so forth. He agreed to this and Mr Tomkins told him that he knew of just such a person—yourself, Patience, although he made no mention of your name or of the fact that you had lived in the house. It is suggested that, if you are agreeable, you might call on the housekeeper and introduce yourself—I feel that her goodwill is important—so that you may allay any fears she may have concerning her position as head of the domestic staff. Presumably you will come under that category. Your working hours have yet to be arranged, also your pay, but, from what I hear, Mr van der Beek is not a mean man. I shall be seeing him when he comes for the keys and will make sure that you are fairly treated.' Mr Bennett held his hands before him as if in prayer. 'I do not need to advise you to keep a low profile, Patience—to be neither seen nor heard should be your aim.'

'Well, I'll do my best, Mr Bennett, and thank you and Mr Tomkins for all your kindness. I am most grateful and a paid job will be more than welcome—I must get some money saved to tide us over until we can let the house or sell it after this Mr van der Beek has gone.' She smiled widely at him. 'Would you like a cup of tea?'

'No, my dear, I must get back and deal with various matters. I should like to call on your aunts tomorrow—there will be papers to sign—which is the best time of day?'

'About eleven o'clock, if you can manage that? May I tell them what you have told me or should you wish to do that yourself tomorrow?'

'Tell them by all means, my dear.' He got to his feet and presently left the house and Patience skipped upstairs on light feet and put away the laundry, humming cheerfully. Now the small outstanding bills could be paid and she could order more coal. She fell to wondering how much money she could expect for her services and then sobered a little at the thought that the housekeeper might take a dislike to her.

She went to the kitchen presently and got a tea-tray ready and, when she heard her aunts' slow progress down the stairs, made the tray ready and carried it in to the sitting-room.

The two old ladies were sitting one each side of the small fire, turning serene faces to her as she went in. They were a handsome pair, upright in their chairs, with identical hairstyles and dressed in similar dark brown dresses which conceded nothing to fashion. They were in fact Patience's great-aunts and her only living relations and she loved them dearly. She poured tea, offered the scones they enjoyed with it and sat down between them. As they always did, they asked her if she had had a pleasant afternoon, the opening which she had been waiting for.

They received her news with dignified delight, although they were both doubtful as to her accepting the job Mr Bennett had offered.

'It seems most unsuitable,' observed Aunt Bessy, the elder of the two ladies. 'Little better than domestic service.'

Patience hastened to reassure her. 'More a secretarial post,' she fibbed boldly, and Aunt Polly, a mere eighty years old and four years her sister's junior, agreed with her in her gentle way.

'It would be nice for Patience to have an outside interest,' she pointed out, 'and money of her own.'

Aunt Bessy, after due thought, conceded this, both old ladies happily unaware that any money their great-niece would earn would probably be swallowed up in the housekeeping purse. Over second cups of tea they pronounced themselves satisfied with the arrangements and willing to receive Mr Bennett when he called on the following day. This settled, they fell to speculating as to their tenant.

'Oh, probably elderly and set in his ways,' said Patience. 'Mr Bennett said that he was very emphatic about having complete quiet in the house while he works. Probably an old despot,' she added, 'but who cares, since he's paying quite a handsome rent and didn't quibble at the idea of hiring me as well?'

Mr Bennett was closeted with her aunts when she got back from the shops on the following morning. She made coffee and was leaving the room when he asked her to stay for a moment . . .

'I have been in touch with Mr van der Beek's secretary,' he told her, 'concerning your employment. He has left the arrangements to her, it seems, and she suggests that you work from ten o'clock until four o'clock with Sundays free—the wages seem generous...' He mentioned a sum which made Patience gasp.

'Heavens, there must be some mistake...'

'No, no. I assure you that it is a fair offer. Cooks earn a great deal nowadays, as do children's nurses and home helps, added to which they have their keep. You will live out, of course, and she suggested that you have three-quarters of an hour for lunch.'

Patience was allowing several pleasant thoughts to race round her sensible head. With money like that she could get Mrs Dodge, who had worked at the house when she and her aunts lived there, to come in for a couple of hours each day and prepare a meal and start to cook it. There would be time enough to do the housework before she went up to the house in the mornings and the whole of a long evening to catch up on the washing and the ironing.

She heard Mr Bennett say, 'I have been asked to telephone back and agree to these terms. References will be required. I will supply one and I will get the Reverend Mr Cuthbertson to supply a second letter. I will see that they are posted this evening and this secretary suggests that you should call and see the housekeeper on the afternoon of her employer's arrival. She emphasises that it is the housekeeper you are to see; on no account is Mr van der Beek to be disturbed. She implied that his household runs on oiled wheels. His housekeeper is called Miss Murch. I have engaged two ladies from here to work daily and old Ned Groom is only too delighted to have work in the garden.' He paused and cleared his throat. 'You have no objection to returning to your old home as a member of the household staff?' he asked delicately.

'None whatever,' declared Patience, a girl of common sense, not giving way to regrets over events which couldn't have been helped anyway once they had occurred. Leaving the nice old house had been a bitter blow but she had never allowed the aunts to see how much she had minded that. They had been marvellous about it, adjusting with dignity to living in the small terraced house they had rented, never complaining. Their one worry had been Patience; they had left the house and their capital to her and now there was nothing. Much though they loved her, they had agreed privately that her chances of marrying were small. For one thing there were few eligible young men in the district, and since she seldom went further afield than Norwich, and that infrequently, there was small chance of there being an opportunity for her to meet a young man, eligible or otherwise. Besides, the dear girl had no looks to speak of; charm and a pretty voice and a nice little figure, if a trifle plump; but men, in the aunts' opinion, liked beauty in a woman, and, failing that, prettiness. They shook their white heads sadly; the dear child tended to be a little too forthright in her talk sometimes, and gentlemen liked to be right about everything even if they weren't, a supposition to which Patience had never subscribed. Her future was a constant worry to them. It was a constant worry to Patience too, although she never said so.

Patience, ready to leave the house for her interview with Miss Murch, stood before the pier-glass in Aunt

Bessy's bedroom and studied her reflection. She looked suitable, she considered, in a pleated tweed skirt, white blouse and her short woollen jacket, all garments she had worn for longer than she cared to remember although of excellent quality, well brushed and pressed. She never wore much make-up; her skin was creamy and as smooth as a child's but she added discreet lipstick and smoothed her hair into even greater neatness. She had left the aunts dozing by the fire, both still a little unsettled at the idea of a Martin going to work in a menial capacity in her own home; it had taken her the intervening days to coax them into fully accepting the idea. She peeped into the sitting-room now, made sure that the fireguard was in place and that they were soundly asleep, and let herself out of the house.

It was ten minutes' walk to her old home, standing as it did half a mile along a narrow lane leading from the village. It should suit the new tenant, she reflected as she stepped out briskly and turned in through the gateposts and up the curved drive. It gave her a pang to see the house again; she had lived there for eleven years, ever since her parents had died in a car accident, and she loved the rather shabby place, timber-framed, its plaster walls pargeted. Its beginnings were some time during the late sixteenth century and it had been added to and altered until it presented a somewhat higgledy-piggledy appearance. The aunts had been born there, for it had been in the Martin family for the last hundred and fifty years; Patience wondered if they would ever live in it again. It seemed unlikely; Mr Bennett had warned them that, if a buyer should take a fancy to it, it would be wise to sell it. It was only after the ladylike battle they had fought

with him that he had agreed to try and let it. Patience
sighed and went round the side of the house to the
tradesmen's entrance. There were lights already in
some of the windows and a Bentley before the front
door, and when she rang the bell it was opened by
Mrs Croft from the village, who welcomed her
warmly. 'Me and Mrs Perch 'as been 'ere all day, Miss
Patience, putting things to rights, as you might say.
You're expected. I'm to take you straight away to Miss
Murch.' She added in a warning whisper, 'Proper ol'
tartar, she is, too.'

Patience followed her along the flagged passage
leading to the kitchen, passing the boot-room, the
pantry, the stillroom and a vast broom-cupboard on
the way. The kitchen was large, rather dark and old-
fashioned. There was a vast porcelain sink, a dresser
taking up most of one wall and any number of cupboards. The scrubbed table in the centre of the room
was capable of seating a dozen persons and there were
Windsor chairs on either side of the Aga—one of the
first models, Aunt Bessy had proudly declared, and
still in fine working order.

The housekeeper's room led off the kitchen and Mrs
Croft pushed open the half-open door. 'Here's Miss
Martin to see you, Miss Murch.' She stood back to
allow Patience to go past her, winked and nodded and
trotted off. She and indeed most of the village had
been warned not to mention the fact that Patience
had lived in the house where she was to be employed,
something they readily agreed to—after all, the
Martins owned the house, didn't they? And the new
tenant was a foreigner, wasn't he? And that Miss
Murch, from what they could see of her as the car
swept through the village, looked an old cross-patch.

Certainly the frowning face turned to her as she went into the room did nothing to raise Patience's hopes. Miss Murch was tall and angular, dressed severely in black, her pepper and salt hair plaited and secured on the top of her head by pins. She had a thin sharp nose, dark eyes and a thin mouth. Patience thought, Oh, dear, and she said, 'Good afternoon, Miss Murch.'

'You are the young woman recommended by the solicitors?' She glanced at the letters on the desk before her; Mr Bennett and the Reverend Mr Cuthbertson had no doubt written suitably. 'Your references are good—I see that you have the same name as the owners of the house.' She paused and looked at Patience.

'It is a common name in these parts, Miss Murch.'

'I believe that Mr van der Beek's secretary has already outlined your duties. It must be understood that you will come to me for instructions; I have kept house for Mr van der Beek for some years and I know exactly how he wishes his home to be run. Any deviation from that will not be tolerated. You will work from ten o'clock until four o'clock with the exception of Sunday, you will have three-quarters of an hour for your midday meal, you may have a cup of coffee during the morning and a cup of tea during the afternoon, and I expect you to work hard. You are already aware of what your wages will be and they will be paid weekly.' She paused but Patience prudently held her tongue and Miss Murch continued, 'You are to answer the telephone, prevent disturbances of any kind at the door and deal with the local tradespeople. It may be necessary from time to time for you to undertake some household tasks. Even in the short time in which we have been here I have become aware that there are very few modern appliances in the house; the bathrooms are old-fashioned and the kitchen quarters are ill equipped.'

Patience bit back rude words. 'I believe the Aga is old, but—but I'm told that it is quite satisfactory.'

Miss Murch gave a ladylike snort. 'I hope that you may be right. Well, that is settled—I shall expect you on Monday morning. Use the side-door; Mr van der Beek is not to be disturbed. Good day to you, Miss Martin.'

I shall hate it, thought Patience, going back to the little terraced house, but it was only for six months, she reflected, and her wages were generous. She would be able to save enough to keep them going while Mr Tomkins looked for a buyer or tenant. She gave the aunts a version of her interview which she knew would satisfy them and went to the kitchen to get the tea.

The aunts went to church in the morning, but Patience for once excused herself. There was a pile of ironing to be done as well as Sunday lunch to cook; she would be busy enough in the morning leaving everything ready for the aunts' lunch and tidying the house.

It was a wild, blustery day. She saw the old ladies safely to the end of the street and into the churchyard and nipped smartly back to get on with the chores uninterrupted. By the time her aunts were back from church she had done everything she needed to do, lunch was ready and the afternoon was hers to do as she wished.

It was barely two o'clock by the time she had washed up the dishes, set the tea ready and made sure that her aunts were settled comfortably. It was raining now and the wind was as strong as ever. A walk, she decided, a good long walk away from the village, along the bridle paths, seldom used these days. She got into her Burberry, a relic of better days and still waterproof, tied a scarf over her head, found a pair of woolly gloves and let herself out of the house. There was no one about but then there wouldn't be—the village would be sitting before the television sets or snoring comfortably before the fire.

She walked briskly, blown along by the wind, past her old home until, half a mile or so along the path, she turned down a bridle path which would lead eventually to the neighbouring village some miles away. She didn't intend to go as far as that, though; there was a short cut after a mile or so which would bring her out on to another path leading back to the village, enabling her to get home before it was dark and her aunts wanted their tea. She squelched along in her wellies, happily engrossed in mental arithmetic which for once was satisfactory, and, that dealt with, she fell to wondering about her job. At least the house would be properly taken care of; Miss Murch didn't look as though she would tolerate slovenly housework and she supposed that since Mr van der Beek was so engrossed in his work it was a good thing he had such an eagle-eyed housekeeper. She amused herself deciding what he would look like. Stout, probably bald, wearing glasses, middle-aged and speaking with a thick accent. A pity she wasn't likely to see him; Miss Murch had seemed determined about that...

She turned off the bridle path, climbed a gate and, keeping to the hedge because of the winter wheat showing green, began to walk its length. The open country stretched all around her, desolate under a

leaden sky with only farm buildings in the distance
to break the empy vastness. Not that Patience thought
of it like that; she loved every stick and stone of it,
just as she knew the names of every person who lived
in Themelswick. Before the death of her parents she
had lived with them at Sheringham where her father
had been a doctor in general practice but in the school
holidays they had often stayed with the aunts at
Themelswick and since there were no other relations
she had been given a home by them when her parents
were killed. They had been kind to her and loving and
had managed, even while their capital dwindled, to
send her to a good boarding-school. When she left
school she stayed at home with the old ladies and ran
the house for them with help from the village and
when they found themselves without money she had
seen to all the tiresome details concerning the renting
of a small house and the letting of their home, as-
suring them that matters were bound to get back to
normal and that they would be able to return to their
old home as soon as things improved. She wasn't sure
how this would come about but it had made it easier
for them to bear leaving the house. Not that they
complained; elderly and forgetful they might be, but
they had a pride which wouldn't allow them to
complain.

Patience was almost at the end of the hedge with
another smaller gate in sight when there was a rus-
tling in the hedge and a smallish dog wormed his way
through it. He was very wet and of no known breed
as far as she could see, but his rough coat gleamed
with good health as well as rain and he was obviously
happy. He pranced around her, uttering little yelps of

pleasure and she stooped to look at the tag on his collar.

'"Basil",' she read. 'What a handsome name for a handsome dog.' The beast licked her rain-wet face and she stroked his damp head. But he had gone again, obedient to a whistle from the other side of the gate, and a moment later the owner of the whistle appeared, not bothering to open the gate but vaulting it lightly despite his size and weight—a giant of a man in a Barbour jacket and cords stuffed into wellington boots. Patience got to her feet as he came towards her. 'Good day. That's a nice dog you've got,' she said. The man might be a stranger but the habit of speaking to everyone she met—as everyone did thereabouts—died hard. He would be one of the guests at the manor, she supposed.

He had drawn level with her now—a handsome man, she noted, but unsmiling. His 'good day' was civil but that was all. He passed her without a second look, striding along the hedge with the dog frisking around his heels. Patience watched him go and, mindful of the time, went on her own way, becoming once more immersed in pleasant speculations as to how best to lay out her wages when she got them, and when she got back to the little terraced house it was to find that her aunts were awake and anxious for their tea. She didn't give the stranger another thought until she was curled up in her bed hours later. 'If he didn't look so cross, he might be a very nice man,' she muttered as she dropped off.

It was strange the following morning, going in through the side-door of her old home, presenting herself in the housekeeper's room exactly on time and waiting to be told what she was to do. If she had had any ideas about not having enough to keep her occupied she was quickly disillusioned; the coal hadn't been delivered, the milkman had got his order wrong and someone was needed to put in extra points to boost what Miss Murch described as woefully inadequate lighting. Patience spent her first hour sorting out these problems, drank her coffee—rather to her surprise—with Miss Murch and then settled down to make a list of the local tradesmen. This done, she was sent to the kitchen garden to find old Ned Groom and ask why he hadn't brought the vegetables up to the house.

'Tiresome ol' woman,' said Ned when she tracked him down in the dilapidated greenhouse, brooding over his cuttings. 'Now these 'ere should do all right—got 'em in just in time.'

'Splendid,' said Patience soothingly. 'Look, Ned, you go on with the cuttings and tell me what I can take. When we left the cabbages were going on well and there must be masses of sprouts unless someone helped themselves—after all, the place has been empty for quite a while.'

'Sprouts enough; take what you want, Miss Patience, and there's carrots ready for pulling and plenty of kale and leeks. It's all a bit untidy like but what do you expect with no one to tend the place?'

She left him grumbling to himself, pulled carrots, leeks and cut a couple of cabbages and bore them back to the kitchen.

'And about time too,' said Miss Murch.

'Well, it will take a little while for Ned to get the garden going again,' Patience pointed out. 'There'll be sprouts tomorrow.'

The day went quickly. Her lunchtime wasn't long enough; as soon as she was paid she would get Mrs Dodge to go for an extra hour each day and get the midday meal for her aunts. They had been waiting placidly for her to get a meal and she had barely had the time to cook omelettes and lay the table before it was time to go back to the house. She hurried back, still hungry, and spent the afternoon trailing Miss Murch round the house, noting down all the things that lady found it essential to replace or add to what she considered to be a woefully ill-equipped household. Patience, who had lived most of her life using wooden spoons and pudding basins and old-fashioned egg whisks, couldn't for the life of her see the sense of all the electrical equipment Miss Murch needed. Mr van der Beek was going to be very out of pocket by the time he had paid for everything, but that of course was his business.

There had been no sign of him; the study door on the other side of the hall had remained shut although of course he could easily have gone in and out several times without her seeing him—her duties carried her all over the house as well as down to the village on an errand for Miss Murch.

She was glad to go home at four o'clock. At Miss Murch's instruction she had laid a tea-tray, pre-sumably for Mr van der Beek, before she went, cut sandwiches of Gentleman's Relish, arranged a fruit cake on a cake stand, and warmed the teapot. Miss Murch nodded approval. 'The electrician will be here tomorrow morning; be sure that you are not late, Patience.'

Patience raced back to the village, got tea for her aunts and herself and sat down thankfully to tell them

about her day, making light of the more menial tasks
she had been given. She suspected that she was being
tried out by Miss Murch and that that lady, formidable in appearance though she was, wasn't as awe-
inspiring as she had at first thought.

By the middle of the week she had found her
bearings. There was plenty for her to do; the phone,
after the first day, rang a great deal, and she had got
quite good at telling whoever it was at the other end
that Mr van der Beek was either not at home, in his
bath, or closeted with his publisher. She varied her
fibs according to the time of day, but took careful
note of the caller's name. She had had strict instructions to fob off any callers but, all the same, each
afternoon before she went home she left a neat list
on the tea-tray.

Mr van der Beek, his notes carefully sorted and the
bare bones of the first chapter of his learned volume
lying before him on his desk after four days' hard
work, laid down his pen and strolled out of the study.
Each morning before his household was stirring he
had let himself out of the house with his dog and
walked until breakfast-time; he walked again in the
evening but so far he hadn't taken much interest in
the house. Miss Murch cooked delicious meals for
him, kept the house quiet and disturbed him not at
all but now he had an urge to look around him.

It was a chilly morning; he would find his way to
the kitchen and ask for his coffee. He stood in the
hall, looking around him, and his eye lighted on the
bowl of winter jasmine set on the wall table. It was
a splash of colour and he wondered who had put it
there. Miss Murch, splendid housekeeper that she was,
wasn't one to waste time arranging flowers. A faint

sound behind him made him turn his head, in time to see a grey skirt disappearing through the dining-room door, with such swiftness that he wondered if he had imagined it. He shrugged huge shoulders, went to the kitchen and had his coffee sitting on the kitchen table while Miss Murch made pastry and then made his way back to the study. He was in the hall when he came face to face with Patience.

CHAPTER TWO

IT WAS Basil who made the first move; he trotted
forward and jumped up at Patience, recognising
someone he had already met and liked. She bent to
pat him, glad of something to do, for Mr van der
Beek's stare was disconcerting.

'Ah, yes,' his voice was cool, 'Basil remembers you.'
His tone implied that he himself did not. 'I take it
you are the—er—general factotum whom Mr Bennett
urged me to employ.'

She didn't allow herself to be disconcerted by his
cold eyes. 'Yes, Mr van der Beek, I'm Patience
Martin.' She added, wishing to be friendly, 'We met
out walking on Sunday afternoon.'

'Did we?' He turned away. 'Don't let me keep you
from your work.'

She put away the table silver she had been cleaning
and went back to the kitchen to make a neat list of
the groceries Miss Murch wanted delivered on the following day. 'Tell that butcher that I want the best
Scotch beef; if he hasn't got it, he need not bother to
send anything else.'

Patience called in on her way home that afternoon
to warn the butcher. 'I know you have excellent meat,
but the housekeeper is determined to find fault with
everything. I don't think she likes living out of
London.'

Mr Crouch leaned his elbows on the counter. 'She's
going to like it even less—there's bad weather on the

26

way, Miss Patience; snow and a nasty east wind. Like as not she'll be holed up there in the house for days on end.'

Mr Crouch was noted for his weather predictions. 'I might get holed up too,' said Patience. 'Just to be on the safe side I think I'll talk to Mrs Dodge...she might have to keep an eye on the aunts.'

'Yes, do that, love. Got plenty of stores up at the house, have they?'

'Enough for a week, but not bread or milk, and there might be power cuts.'

'Well, you bear it in mind. Remember that winter four years back—you was all cut off for days—us as well—real blizzard that were and no mistake.'

'It's only half a mile away from the village,' observed Patience.

'Might just as well be ten miles when there's drifts.' Mr Crouch wiped down the counter. 'I've a tasty pair of chops if you fancy them to give Miss Martin and her sister...'

Patience took the chops and herself off home to the aunts, waiting with ladylike patience for their tea.

She broached the subject of possible bad weather to Miss Murch on the next day.

'There's nothing on the weather forecast,' said Miss Murch. 'I shall want some carrots from the garden; Mr van der Beek likes a carrot.'

Patience didn't think that Mr van der Beek would enjoy anything as homely as a carrot but she went and found old Ned, who filled her trug and remarked gloomily that there was bad weather on the way and how was he supposed to get at the cabbages and leeks if they got snowed up?

'Miss Murch says there's nothing on the weather forecast . . .'

Old Ned's snort dismissed Miss Murch. 'And what do she know about it, eh?' He patted a string of splendid onions with a loving hand. 'You mark my words . . .'

Patience, who had more faith in old Ned and Mr Crouch than the weathermen, had another go at Miss Murch. 'This house has been cut off during bad weather,' she volunteered, not mentioning that she and her aunts had been cut off too. 'The snow drifts badly here—it's rather flat, you see.'

'Then what are the snowploughs for?' asked Miss Murch witheringly. 'This may be the back of beyond but presumably it is entitled to the same public services as those enjoyed by more civilised parts.'

Patience gave up and went away to answer the doorbell. Someone from a firm in Norwich wanting to know if the owner of the house would like double glazing.

'Well, he's not here—away for a few days.' Patience, hardened to telling fibs, after a little pause added, 'If you want to come again it would save a lot of time if you phoned first. He's not often at home.'

She smiled kindly at the man, who looked as though he could have done with a warm drink. On her own she would undoubtedly have given him one. 'You could try the vicarage if you haven't called there already . . .'

He went away quite cheerful; she was sure the vicar couldn't afford double glazing but she was just as sure that the man would be given a cup of tea. Selling double glazing in January was no way to earn a living; she thought of Mr van der Beek, secure in the cosy fastness of his study, having regular meals and earning fabulous sums just by sitting at a desk and writing.

Mr van der Beek was indeed sitting at his desk, but he wasn't writing. To his annoyance his powerful brain was refusing to concentrate upon transcribing his notes into plain English—interlarded with Latin medical terms of course—instead, he found his thoughts wandering towards his general factotum. A mouselike creature if ever there was one, he reflected, and surely with that ordinary face and mouselike hair she didn't need to dress like a mouse? Her eyes were beautiful, though; he reflected for a few moments on the length and curl of her eyelashes. She had a charming voice too... He picked up his pen and summarily dismissed her from his mind.

The following morning when Patience went down to the kitchen garden she found old Ned stacking carrots, leeks and turnips in neat piles in the greenhouse. 'Them turnips will be tough,' he pointed out, 'seeing as 'ow there weren't no one to dig 'em up at the proper time. They'll bake, though, and likely keep you going while the snow lasts.'

Patience didn't argue with him; she could see that the weather was changing with sullen clouds creeping in from the sea and a nasty cold wind.

'It'll be snowing by the morning,' said old Ned.

He was right; there was already a light covering when she got up and the still dark sky had a nasty yellow tinge to it. She was glad that she had seen Mrs Dodge, who lived close by and even in very bad weather would be able to get to the aunts. She had stocked up the kitchen cupboard too. She made sure that the house was warm and her aunts suitably clad and fed before setting out for the house; the weather report had mentioned light snow in East Anglia and for the moment, at any rate, it was quite right; the snow drifted down, occasionally blown into a flurry by a gust of east wind, cold enough to take her breath. It was pleasant to enter the warm house and sniff the fragrance of bacon, still lingering in the kitchen after Miss Murch had cooked Mr van der Beek's breakfast.

'You'd better fetch the vegetables while you've got your outdoor things on,' said Miss Murch, adding grudgingly that it wasn't a nice morning.

Old Ned in mittens and an overcoat was in the greenhouse. 'No good me staying 'ere,' he told Patience. 'I've picked some sprouts; you'd better take 'em with you. What's it to be today?'

'Onions and carrots, but I'll take the sprouts and a cabbage, in case I can't get down tomorrow.' She added hopefully, 'Perhaps the snow won't last.'

To which remark her companion gave a derisive cackle of laughter.

It snowed gently all day but not alarmingly so, Mrs Croft and Mrs Perch came and went, and the house, polished and hoovered and delightfully warm, made nonsense of the chilly weather outside. Patience went home at four o'clock and, being country born and bred, sniffed the air with a knowledgeable little nose— there was more snow on the way. She called at Mr Crouch's shop and bought braising steak and plenty of bacon; a really large casserole would last them two days and only need warming up...

As she went out of the shop the Bentley whispered past with Mr van der Beek at the wheel—so he'd been away all day. She frowned, thinking of the care with which she and Mrs Croft and Mrs Perch had moved silently around the house so that he shouldn't be disturbed—and all for nothing. She stood looking after the car and Mr van der Beek watched her in his side-mirror. She was wearing the old Burberry again and a woolly cap in some useful colour pulled down over her hair. Really, he thought irritably, the girl had no dress sense.

It was still snowing when she left the little house in the morning and the sky was ominously dark. She had left a substantial casserole cooked and ready, peeled potatoes for two days, and left everything as ready as possible for her aunts just in case she wouldn't be able to get home at midday. Mrs Dodge would go in, of course, and almost everyone in the village knew where she was; all the same she felt a faint unease, for the wind was getting strong, blowing the snow into spirals going in every direction.

The worsening weather seemed to have no effect upon the occupants of the house. Patience, unaware that Mr van der Beek had been out early with Basil, thought that probably he had no idea how wintry it could be in Norfolk at that time of the year, and, as for Miss Murch, she had no interest in the outside world; she was already in the kitchen making marmalade.

The weather became steadily worse as the morning wore on and Mrs Croft and Mrs Perch left earlier than usual, declaring that the school would surely close early because of the weather and the children would be sent home. Patience, taking a look out of the window, decided not to try and struggle home and back again—in less than an hour it wouldn't be possible and, as if to underline her decision, the wind increased with a quite frightening suddenness.

By mid-afternoon it was dark and the wind was howling around the house. Patience, bidden by Miss Murch to draw the curtains, could see nothing but a curtain of snowflakes outside and when the lights began to flicker and the wind increased she went round the house, setting candlesticks and matches at strategic points.

Miss Murch, coming upon her setting an old fashioned candelabrum on the hall table, remarked tartly that anyone would think that she had done it all before, to which Patience made no reply.

Wrapped in the Burberry and the woolly cap, she knew before she had reached the end of the drive that getting back to the village would be impossible. There was a hollow in the lane a hundred yards from the house and she could see that the drifts were already head-high. Almost blown off her feet, she was half blinded by the snow and so she went back to the house.

Miss Murch eyed her sopping figure. 'You'll have to stay the night,' she pronounced. 'You can telephone to your home.'

'We aren't on the phone, but it's all right, my aunts won't worry; they would know that once the snow started drifting there wouldn't be a way back.'

'This Godforsaken place,' declared Miss Murch crossly. 'Get those wet things off; since you're here you can help me with Mr van der Beek's dinner.'

The kitchen was warm and smelled deliciously of something roasting in the Aga. 'You had better have the room opposite mine,' said Miss Murch. 'You can have one of my nightgowns and then we can make up the bed presently. We'll have our supper once Mr van der Beek has had his dinner.'

The electricity wavered for another half-hour and then went out. Patience went around lighting candles and the oil-lamps her aunts had always kept handy. The dining-room looked quite cosy when she had set candles on the table, but she didn't linger; she had heard the subdued roar from Mr van der Beek when the power was cut, and he might not be in the best of tempers. She went to the lamp-room behind the kitchen and found another oil-lamp; the moment he went into the dining-room she would nip into the study and light it.

Miss Murch took the dinner in, tapping discreetly on the study door to let him know that it was served. Patience heard his voice, coldly annoyed, as she slid out of the kitchen and into the study. There was a splendid fire burning; by its light she lit the lamp and set it on his desk.

She itched to tidy the piles of papers strewn around. How, she wondered, did he ever find anything in all that muddle?

She had her supper with Miss Murch later that evening, listening politely to that lady's accounts of the convenience and comfort of Mr van der Beek's house in London. 'He has a house in Holland as well,' she told Patience. 'He visits there from time to time. He is, as you doubtless know, very well thought of throughout the medical profession.'

Patience murmured politely, and helped with the washing-up while Miss Murch sang the praises of the dish-washing machine at the London house, and retired to her room. It was close to Miss Murch's at the back of the house and the wind howled against the window, its glass peppered with snowflakes. Patience pulled the curtains, had a very hot bath in the rather antiquated bathroom and jumped into bed. She had experienced weather like this several times and it was unlikely to disturb her sleep. She set the alarm clock Miss Murch had thoughtfully given her for seven o'clock and went to sleep.

It was the dead of night when she woke and she knew at once what it was that had awakened her. One of the shutters in the unused scullery beyond the kitchen had broken loose and was banging against the wall. Then she lay and listened to it for a few minutes and decided to go down and see if she could close it. She lighted her candle and crept along the passage, pausing at Miss Murch's door. Judging by the snores coming from her room, Miss Murch hadn't been bothered by the noise. Patience remembered uneasily that Mr van der Beek's bedroom, at the other side of the house, while not above the kitchen wing, was on the same side. She pattered silently on bare feet down the stairs, across the hall and through the baize door to the kitchen.

Mr van der Beek's sleep, untroubled by the violence of the wind, was disturbed by the regular banging of the shutter, the kind of noise which would prevent even the most placid person from dozing off. He got into his dressing-gown and slippers by the light of his torch and went to the head of the stairs, just in time to see the faint glow of Patience's candle dwindle from the hall. Following it quietly, he was in time to see Patience, shrouded in one of Miss Murch's winceyette nighties, cross the kitchen and open the door leading to the various rooms beyond... She paused on her way to stoop and pat Basil curled up before the Aga. Mr van der Beek, standing in the kitchen doorway, watched her, the corners of his thin mouth twitching. Miss Murch's nightie covered her from just under her chin to her heels and beyond for there was a good deal of surplus trailing behind her, the full sleeves she had rolled up to allow her hands to emerge and her hair hung in a mousy cloud halfway down her back.

Mr van der Beek coughed politely and hushed Basil who had got up to greet him, delighted to have some company.

Patience nearly dropped the candle. She turned slowly and said severely, 'I might have screamed, Mr van der Beek.'

'Oh, no, you're not the screaming kind,' he told her. 'If you were you would be upstairs now with your head under the bedclothes. Is it a loose shutter somewhere?'

'In the pantry, I think, or the scullery. Through here . . .' She led the way, much too concerned about the noise to think about the strange appearance she presented. It was a loose shutter in the scullery. Mr van der Beek secured it and looked around him.

'What an extremely dreary place,' he remarked, and without looking at her added, 'I am chilled to the bone; let us have a hot drink before we return to our beds.'

'Well, that would be nice,' said Patience, 'but I'm not sure—I mean, I haven't got a dressing-gown . . .' She had gone rather red but she gave him a steady look.

'My dear young lady, no dressing-gown could cover you as adequately as the garment in which you presently appear to be smothered. Miss Murch's, I gather?'

He had led the way back to the kitchen and opened up the Aga and filled a kettle. 'Tea?' he asked.

Patience thrust back her sleeves once more and crossed to the dresser, collecting cups and saucers, spoons, the tea caddy and a tray with the ease of long custom. As she came back with the milk jug and sugar bowl Mr van der Beek, watching the kettle come to the boil, remarked quietly, 'You are familiar with this house, are you not, Miss Martin? Was it your home?'

'Oh, how did you know?' She paused on her way to the table. 'I didn't—I didn't mean to deceive you, you know, only Mr Bennett thought you might need someone to give a hand and as I knew where everything was and the tradespeople . . .'

'You have no need to apologise. I am sure you are worth your weight in gold. Do I have to call you Miss Martin?'

'Oh, no, no. That wouldn't do at all. My name's Patience.'

He nodded. 'And the two ladies who come each day to work here? They know who you are?'

'Oh, yes. They used to work here while my aunts lived in this house, only not for some time now; for the last few months we managed very nicely without anyone.'

He poured water into the teapot. 'Your aunts are elderly?' He knew the answer to that but all the same he waited to hear what she would say.

'We closed up most of the rooms.' She spoke with a touch of defiance and he smiled.

'Come and drink your tea. Are we likely to be snowed in?'

'Oh, yes. The ploughs will come, of course, but they clear the main roads first so it will be a day or two.'

'Will we be able to get through to the village?' he asked idly.

'Not until the wind dies down and we can dig our way out. The lane dips and there is always a drift every time there. Well,' she added fairly, 'there are drifts all over the place but the one in the lane is particularly deep.'

'So we may be isolated for several days?'

'I expect so.' She added kindly, 'But that will be nice for you; you wanted to be very quiet, didn't you? And no one is likely to call; the phone will be down, it always is, and of course the postman can't get here.'

'An interesting prospect. I trust there is enough coal and wood to keep us warm?'

She nodded and said in her practical way, 'Yes, I got old Ned to bring some logs up to the boot-room and there is plenty of coal, and if we run short we can live in the kitchen.'

Mr van der Beek sighed; living in the kitchen was something he would prefer not to do, and besides he would be hindered from his writing. He drank the last of his tea and watched her stifle a yawn. 'Go back to bed, Patience, and get some sleep. I'll blow out the candles.'

She wished him goodnight and, clutching the surplus folds of her nightgown, made her way back to her room. It was cold there after the kitchen but she was too tired to mind that. She was already asleep within minutes.

It was still dark when she got up and the snow had faltered to occasional flurries driven by the wind. She dressed, wound her hair into a neat bun and went downstairs to the kitchen. The Aga might be old but it still worked; she added coal, turned up the heat and set a kettle on to boil. Miss Murch would be down presently and both she and Mr van der Beek would expect tea. There was no sign of Basil, but presently she heard him barking. Perhaps he had got shut out— she went through the scullery and past the boot-room and opened the old door which led to the garden. Here it had been somewhat sheltered from the wind so that the snow hadn't drifted although it was several inches deep. She poked her head out cautiously, her breath taken by the icy air, and was rewarded by the sight of Mr van der Beek shovelling snow, making a narrow path towards the woodshed. He appeared to be enjoying himself, tossing great shovelfuls to one side as though they were feathers. He had a splendid pair of shoulders, thought Patience, watching him, and, dressed as he was in a great baggy sweater with trousers stuffed into his boots, he didn't look at all like the austere man whom she spent her days avoiding.

It was Basil who saw her and came romping back to say hello and although Mr van der Beek didn't look up he called over one shoulder, 'I should like a cup of tea...'

'Well, you shall have one if you come into the kitchen now,' said Patience tartly, 'and wipe your boots and leave them on the mat.'

She didn't wait for an answer but went back to the kitchen, made the tea and set out a small tray ready to carry to the study. As soon as he had had it and gone upstairs to make himself presentable for his breakfast she would nip in and get the fire raked out and lighted.

Basil came prancing in, delighted with the weather, and his master with him, looking meek in his socks. 'I'll take the tray through to the study,' said Patience.

'Indeed you will not. It's freezing there. I'll have it here. Where's Miss Murch?'

'I expect she will be down presently to cook your breakfast.' She picked up the teapot and he put three mugs down on the table.

'Let's not be dainty. I like two lumps of sugar. Is there a towel I can use to rub Basil dry?'

'Behind the door. I'll fetch a clean one for us to use.'

Miss Murch, coming into the kitchen, paused in the doorway. Her, 'Good morning, Mr van der Beek,' was glacial, but he didn't appear to notice that.

'I'm going to shave,' he told her cheerfully, 'and I'll have my breakfast here where it's warm—twenty minutes?' He gave her a charming smile, whistled to Basil and went out of the room.

'I made a pot of tea,' said Patience. 'Would you like a cup, Miss Murch? The Aga's going nicely and Mr van der Beek has cleared a path to the woodshed so there'll be plenty of coal and logs. Would you like me to see to the fire in the study first?'

'Well, since there's no one else. We had better have our breakfast when Mr van der Beek has finished his. If you could light the study fire it would soon be warm enough for him.' She sounded almost apologetic.

Patience got into the apron Mrs Perch used when she came to work, collected bucket, shovel, paper and kindling, and went off to the study. It was getting light now; she drew back the curtains to find that the snow had heaped itself up against the windows so that she had to stand firmly on tiptoe in order to see out;

really she might just as well have left the curtains drawn ...

She had a nice fire going and was sitting back on her heels admiring it when Mr van der Beek came in.

'What the hell are you doing?' he wanted to know, and she glanced up in surprise; it didn't sound like him at all.

She said in the kind of voice she might have used to a child who needed something explained, 'I'm making sure that the fire is going to burn.'

'I can see that for myself. In future, until this crisis is over, I shall light the fires, fetch the wood and the coals and dispose of the ashes.'

Patience looked at him with interest. 'Do you know how?' she asked, and at his icy look added, 'Oh, don't look like that, I don't mean to be rude but I dare say in your home you don't need to lift a finger.'

'You consider that I am a man of leisure?'

'Well, I hadn't really thought about it, but I've got eyes—you drive a lovely car and Miss Murch says you are very successful—I dare say you lead a very pleasant life with lots of friends and theatres and so on.'

Mr van der Beek, slavishly revered by those students lucky enough to be under his tuition, tirelessly devoted to his work and his patients, so generous with both his time and his money, agreed meekly.

Patience laid another piece of coal exactly where it was most needed and got up. 'It's very kind of you to offer,' she told him gratefully, 'but if you aren't used to doing it, lighting a fire can be very tiresome.'

'And you're good at it?' His voice was bland. 'What else are you good at, Patience?'

'Me?' She thought for a moment. 'Why—nothing much—I can cook and mend things—sew and knit—change plugs, mend fuses, that kind of thing.'

'You have no wish to do anything else?' He spoke casually with just the right amount of interest.

'I'm not clever and I'm plain—Aunt Bessy says I'm the plainest girl she has ever seen, but if I could be clever and charming and pretty I'd like to spend a week in London going to the theatres and the kind of restaurants where there are candles on the tables and waiters and the menu is in French—and shopping of course... Your breakfast will be ready, Mr van der Beek.' Her voice was all of a sudden brisk. 'Now there's a fire I can bring a tray in here...'

'I actually said I would have my breakfast in the kitchen,' he reminded her, and now he didn't sound friendly any more.

He was adamant that Miss Murch and Patience should have breakfast with him too but he was no longer casually friendly; the conversation was strictly businesslike and concerned the possibility of being snowed in for a further day or so and how to make the best of it. 'Close the rooms we don't need,' he told Miss Murch. 'This kitchen is the warmest place in the house; we can eat here—the study and the small sitting-room will be all right with fires. Are there enough candles and lamps?'

Miss Murch looked at Patience. 'Plenty of candles but there's not a great deal of oil left,' said Patience. 'We could keep the lamps for the study and take the candles with us when we go from room to room; they'll last ages that way.'

'Food?'

Miss Murch replied with dignity. 'I trust I am a sufficiently good housekeeper to ensure a fully adequate supply of food for several days at least, and that of course over and above my normal store of groceries.'

'There's plenty of greenstuff in the greenhouse,' said Patience. 'If Mr van der Beek could dig a path I can go and collect as much as we're likely to need before it's frozen solid.'

'Mr van der Beek has better ways of employing his time,' observed Miss Murch sharply.

Mr van der Beek took another slice of toast and buttered it lavishly. 'Indeed I have,' he agreed. 'On the other hand can you, in all fairness, conceive of Patience digging her way through a snowdrift? There's not enough of her.'

Patience bore the scrutiny of two pairs of eyes with equanimity. 'I am very strong,' she observed in a matter-of-fact voice.

'The exercise will do me good,' said Mr van der Beek in the kind of voice with which one couldn't argue.

It took him the whole morning with the briefest of intervals while he drank the hot coffee which Patience, wrapped in one of Miss Murch's cardigans on top of her own woolly, took to the garden door.

'You're doing very nicely, Mr van der Beek,' she said encouragingly. 'There's a little dip just before you get to the greenhouse; take care you don't trip up.'

A giant of a man, rock-steady on his large feet, he nevertheless thanked her politely for the warning.

It was very cold and the wind, which had died down, started up again with renewed ferocity. Patience, scuttling around the house, stoking the study fire, making beds and cleaning vegetables at Miss Murch's bidding, worried about the aunts. True, the little house was easy to keep warm and Mrs Dodge had promised to keep an eye on them. The news, on Miss Murch's portable radio in the kitchen, held out little hope of the weather improving for at least twenty-four hours, perhaps longer.

'Really, I do not know what the world is coming to,' observed Miss Murch crossly. 'How am I to get fresh meat in this weather?'

It wasn't worth answering. 'As soon as I can get to the village I shall need to go and see if my aunts are all right, Miss Murch...'

'At the same time you can call at the butcher.'

There was no point in telling her that Mr Crouch got his meat for the most part from local markets and farms and transport would be difficult for several days.

Miss Murch, despite her ill humour, contrived a delicious soup, cheese and onion pasties and a large pot of coffee. Mr van der Beek, glowing with good health and a certain smugness, ate hugely and went away to his study. 'A cup of tea at four o'clock,' he asked, 'and on no account am I to be disturbed until dinner—at half-past seven if that is possible, Miss Murch?'

He walked away without waiting for an answer.

Patience cleared the table and began to wash the dishes. 'It is ridiculous that there is no dishwasher,' remarked Miss Murch, making no effort to give a hand. 'I shall lie down for a time, Patience; I have a headache.'

'Shall I bring you a cup of tea just before four o'clock?'

'Yes, thank you. I find this snow very trying.'

Left to herself, Patience saw to the Aga, cast an eye on the fire in the sitting-room and looked out of the window. It was snowing again.

She laid a tray for Mr van der Beek's tea and another for Miss Murch and herself and took herself off to the sitting-room, to curl up before the fire with the only book she could find—*Beeton's Household Management*. It made interesting reading and was profusely illustrated with coloured plates of mouth-watering food.

Miss Murch didn't look very well when she took her a cup of tea but she came down to the kitchen presently and cut delicate sandwiches of Gentleman's Relish to add to the pot of tea on Mr van der Beek's tray.

'Don't go in before you're told to,' she admonished Patience, 'and don't stop and talk either. Just put the tray down and come away at once.'

Patience's gentle tap was answered by an impatient voice bidding her enter and when she did so he snapped, 'You may look like a mouse, but you don't have to behave like one—I don't bite.'

'I should hope not, indeed,' said Patience briskly. 'I was told to make no noise and not to come in until I was told...' She added kindly, 'I dare say you're busy with your book—is it about surgery?'

'Er—some aspects of it, yes—a reference book...'

'Like Mrs Beeton's cookery book, I dare say, full of instructions about the best way to cook food, written by an expert.'

Mr van der Beek's eyelids drooped over an amused gleam. 'If that is a compliment, Patience, thank you. I cannot compete with Mrs Beeton in her own field, but I venture to admit to being moderately well known in my own.'

Miss Murch's headache had returned; Patience, taking care not to usurp that lady's authority, did as much as she could to help her so that by the time dinner was ready there was an appetising meal on the table.

Mr van der Beek was in the sitting-room by the fire, with Basil at his feet. He had taken the trouble to change into a collar and tie and a good tweed jacket, and Patience, sent to fetch him to the kitchen, was made aware of her own appearance. With an eye to the weather she had come to work in a thick tweed skirt and an equally thick sweater over a shirt blouse and she had nothing with her to make this prosaic outfit more becoming, but at least her hair, strained back into a large bun, was tidy, and she had powdered her nose.

Miss Murch had done them proud, there were leeks in a french dressing, *boeuf bourguignon* and sautéd potatoes and an egg custard with a variety of cheeses to round off this heartening fare. Mr van der Beek made polite conversation and made no comment at Miss Murch's lack of appetite; only when the meal was finished did he ask casually, 'You've got a headache, Miss Murch?'

'A slight one, sir.'

'May I suggest a bed, a warm hot-water bottle and a hot drink? I'll let you have some paracetamol. If you don't feel better in the morning, stay in bed— there's nothing like a day in bed to discourage a cold.'

He smiled kindly at her and bade her goodnight before turning to Patience. 'Will you see that Miss

Murch does just that?' He glanced at the table. 'These can wait for the time being.'

So Patience filled a hot-water bottle, urged Miss Murch upstairs to her cold bedroom and went away to get her a hot drink. It would have to be tea; the milk was running low. Miss Murch was in bed by the time she got back; she handed the pills, fetched a glass of water for the night and waited while the hot drink was swallowed. 'I'll pop in tomorrow morning,' she said. 'I'm sorry you're not feeling well; a good night's sleep will probably put it right.'

When she got back to the kitchen it was to find the dishes washed and the kitchen more or less tidy. She was standing rather aimlessly when Mr van der Beek put his head round the door. 'Go to bed, Patience. I'll see to the Aga. Good night.'

It didn't turn out to be a good night, though.

CHAPTER THREE

PATIENCE was awakened just after one o'clock by Miss Murch, standing by her bed and thumping her on the shoulder. She held a lighted candle and in its meagre light her appearance to the sleepy Patience was alarming.

'I am cold,' snarled Miss Murch. 'Get me a hot drink and refill my bottle, this house will be my death...'

Patience nipped out of bed and put a comforting arm around the housekeeper. It was startling to feel how hot she was despite her shivers. 'Come back to bed,' she coaxed. 'I'll be back in no time with a drink and a hot-water bottle; I'll bring a spare blanket too...'

She was creeping down the stairs when Mr van der Beek loomed on the landing.

'Now what?' He sounded resigned. 'Miss Murch?'

'Yes. She says she's cold but she feels very hot. I'm going to get her a hot drink and fill a bottle...'

'You have nothing on your feet.'

'Well, I didn't bring an overnight bag with me, did I?' She spoke reasonably, not waiting for an answer as she skimmed along to the kitchen.

When she got back to Miss Murch's room, Mr van der Beek was there, sitting on the side of the bed, looking at the thermometer in his hand. His expression told her nothing and he said cheerfully, 'Well, Miss Murch, you have a touch of flu. You will stay in bed for a few days until you feel more the thing

47

and we will nurse you. I am going to give you some
tablets which you will take but first I am going to give
you an injection—an antibiotic which will give the
tablets a boost.' He looked at Patience. 'More pillows
and another blanket?' he asked.

She soon got them off her own bed and together
they propped up Miss Murch, and, when he had given
her the injection, tucked her up warmly.

Mr van der Beek cast a brief glance at Patience.
'Borrow Miss Murch's slippers and dressing-gown,'
he told her, 'or you'll be in bed too. Go down and
get a cup of tea. I'll be down in a few minutes. We
have to talk.'

Miss Murch's dressing-gown was red and woolly
and several sizes too large; so were the slippers but
their warmth was bliss. Patience, mindful of the
slippers, trod carefully down to the kitchen, trailing
her garments behind her. She put on the kettle, talking
to Basil, curled up cosily before the Aga, arranged
mugs, the teapot and sugar on the table and, when
she heard Mr van der Beek's steady tread on the stairs,
made the tea.

It was only then that she realised that he hadn't yet
been to his bed, for he was still fully dressed, which
perhaps accounted for his impersonal manner. He
pulled out a chair and told her to sit down and went
to sit opposite to her at the table.

'Miss Murch won't be on her feet for a few days,'
he told her. 'Can you cope? I'll see to the fires, we
will live and eat here in this kitchen and share Miss
Murch between us. I fancy she will be a handful. Go
through the cupboards and see how we are off for
food—you'll have to do the cooking.'

Patience nodded and drank her tea, longing for her bed. She looked ridiculous, reflected Mr van der Beek, with her head sticking out of Miss Murch's high-necked nightgown, her hands engulfed in the dressing-gown's sleeves. Her hair was a bird's nest—a very clean bird's nest, though, framing her tired face.

'Go to bed,' he told her and took the hot-water bottle she had brought down for herself and filled it from the kettle. 'I shall look in on Miss Murch presently but she should sleep soundly until the morning. I shall leave her door open—is there a bell . . . ?'

'In the dining-room. I'll fetch it.'

'No, no, you go to bed. I'll bring it with me presently. Goodnight, Patience.'

He had got up to open the door for her and, as she went past, said with wry amusement, 'We mustn't make a habit of this, must we?'

She mumbled a reply and made her way to her room, where she had to make her bed again, creeping to and fro fetching more pillows and a blanket from the linen cupboard on the landing. Miss Murch, she was thankful to see, was asleep . . . She left her own door open and got into bed, hugging the hot-water bottle, and fell asleep at once. She had found some night lights and left one burning on the bedside table and presently, by its feeble light, Mr van der Beek, on his way to cast a professional eye over Miss Murch, studied her sleeping face, puzzled as to why he should find it interesting. He shrugged his shoulders and went to look at his housekeeper and then at last took himself off to bed.

It was snowing again in the morning. Patience put on all the clothes she had, made sure that Miss Murch was still sleeping and that the bell was within her reach

and went downstairs. It was still early but Mr van der
Beek was already in the kitchen, wearing a thick
sweater, raking the Aga and pouring on the coal. They
had a cup of tea before he went off to make a fire in
the study while she got breakfast. There was still
plenty of food in the house; she made porridge,
although there was no milk to spare—what there was
must be saved for Miss Murch—and fried bacon and
slices of bread. There were still eggs but they again
might be needed for Miss Murch. There was, however,
butter, marmalade and plenty of coffee. She was just
ready when Mr van der Beek came back, washed his
hands at the sink and sat down at the table.

'I'll have to clear the paths again but first I'll take
a look at Miss Murch; can you wash her and so forth
presently? Give her as much to drink as she can
manage.' He eyed his black coffee. 'No milk?'

'Enough for Miss Murch. There are a few eggs too
and I can make a jelly...'

'Good. What about us?' He was eating his porridge with every sign of enjoyment.

'Soup for lunch—I'll just have to make some
bread...'

'Can you make bread too?'

'Well, yes. It's quite easy. I thought we might have
that chicken in the freezer—I can casserole it and Miss
Murch can have some sieved.'

'That takes care of today.' He smiled at her across
the table. She looked tired and her hair was pulled
back far too severely. There was no need to make
herself more homely than she already was. He
frowned; homely wasn't the right word—with eyes like
hers she could never be that. Dressed in something
pretty and with her hair less severely treated she could

be quite attractive... He finished his bacon, swallowed the rest of the coffee and got up. 'I'll take a quick look upstairs and then go and see to the paths. Do we need coal and wood?'

'There's some in the boot-room but not enough for tonight.'

He was back presently with the hot bottle for re-filling. 'Miss Murch is awake,' he told her. 'Take these up as you go, I'll take her a cup of tea and sit her up in bed. Her temperature is down slightly. I'll give her her tablet. When you've washed her and tidied her bed and so on, give her another drink—anything she fancies. She should sleep again for a while.'

He went away again, leaving her to wonder how Miss Murch would react to her employer taking her cups of tea and shaking up her pillows.

Miss Murch wasn't well enough to care who did what. She submitted to having her face and hands washed and being put into a clean nightgown and lay submissively while Patience made the bed around her and fetched her a warm drink. Thankfully she fell asleep again almost at once and Patience was able to go back to the kitchen and clear away the breakfast, wash up and clean the kitchen and then start on her breadmaking. There was flour enough and dried yeast among the housekeeper's store; she made a dough, set the loaves to rise and put the kettle on once more. Since the oven was just right, she made a batch of scones, opened a tin of treacle and made a treacle tart. The scones were ready and smelling delicious when Mr van der Beek, obediently in socks, came for his coffee. He sat down at the table and the winged nostrils of his handsome nose flared. 'Something smells appetising. May we eat it?'

Patience smiled and poured their coffee. 'Scones. I'll take them out of the oven if you'd like one.'

She buttered half a dozen lavishly and set the plate between them, found a bone for Basil to gnaw on the rug before the Aga, and sat down to drink her own coffee. 'When would you like your lunch, Mr van der Beek?' she wanted to know, watching the scones disappear.

'One o'clock?' He glanced at his wristwatch. 'I'm going to do some work. Let me know if you need me for anything.'

Patience had her hands full for the rest of the morning; Miss Murch rang the bell continuously and not only for more hot-water bottles and another hot drink but to enquire if Patience had planned a suitable meal for Mr van der Beek and, if so, was she capable of cooking it to his satisfaction?

Patience made soothing noises; if he didn't like the food he could go hungry, she thought privately. Miss Murch pampered him—bread and cheese would do him no harm...

Which was what he got for his lunch but since the bread was fresh from the oven and there was butter as well as cheese, and onion soup besides, he had no cause to grumble. Not that he did; indeed, he ate most of one loaf, declaring that she was a treasure and that he was glad to have discovered her.

'But you didn't,' declared Patience, outspoken as usual. 'Mr Bennett hired me on your behalf—you didn't know I was here until we met in the hall.'

'Don't split hairs,' he begged her, and went back to his study.

She took him tea and a plate of scones at four o'clock; he didn't look up when she went in and his 'thank you' was uttered in an absent-minded voice. She went away soundlessly; he was deep in bones or internal organs and she supposed that instead of asking him to fetch more coal, which she had intended to do, she had better carry the buckets to and fro herself. The snow had stopped but there was still no sign of a thaw.

The chicken casserole had been on the Aga for hours, she had peeled the potatoes, and the treacle tart only needed to be eaten; with a minute to spare she went to her own room to tidy herself and met Mr van der Beek coming from Miss Murch's room.

'An improvement,' he told her. 'A couple more days in bed and we shall be able to get her down to the kitchen—I'll carry one of the easy-chairs in and she can sit there and bear you company.' He studied her face. 'You look tired...'

'I am tired. Dinner is for seven-thirty, Mr van der Beek.'

'Splendid. We need a drink first. Come down to the kitchen...'

'There are several things which need to be done,' she told him.

She sounded peevish and he said at once, 'Ah, coal and wood to fetch—I'll see to that.'

'I've already done so,' her voice was cold as well as peevish, 'otherwise the fires go out.'

'Why didn't you ask me?'

'I intended to, but it hardly seemed the right moment when I took in your tea.'

'My poor girl,' he bent his head and kissed her gently on her cheek, 'how thoughtless I have been.'

The kiss had been comforting but she didn't allow it to go to her head.

She said matter-of-factly, 'I dare say if you have people to do things for you you don't need to bother about the running of a house, cooking and washing and ironing and dusting and hoovering.'

He admitted that it was indeed the case. 'Come down as soon as you can and we will work something out.'

Miss Murch needed to be washed and her bed remade, bottles refilled once again and her hair brushed and plaited. She wasn't a cheerful patient but Patience supposed that if she felt as ill as the housekeeper she would be just as gloomy and tiresome.

She went downstairs presently, her hair pinned back severely from her face, wishing that she had something to wear other than the skirt and sweater. Her spirits would have sunk even lower if she had known that Mr van der Beek, turning to look at her as she went into the kitchen, thought exactly the same thing.

The casserole eaten and mugs of milkless coffee on the table, Mr van der Beek produced a notebook and a pencil. 'Now tell me absolutely everything that has to be done each day and that includes looking after Miss Murch.'

She took him at his word and really the list was quite a formidable one. He studied it for a moment. 'I'll leave the housework to you,' he said finally. 'I'll wash the dishes, fetch the coal and wood, and, when we can get to them, the vegetables. I'll engage to keep Miss Murch supplied with hot-water bottles and I'll set the table for meals and see to the Aga and the fire in my study.'

'What about your book?'

'I'd like the afternoon free of any interruptions; I can work again after dinner in the evening. Miss Murch should be settled by then.'

It was on the tip of her tongue to ask if she should sit like Cinderella in the kitchen until bedtime but all she said was, 'Very well, Mr van der Beek.'

In fact the kitchen was delightfully warm. Once the dishes had been washed and Miss Murch had been settled for the night and Mr van der Beek had shut himself in the study, Patience curled up in one of the Windsor chairs by the Aga. It wasn't possible to read by the light of the one candle she had allowed herself; besides, unless she went and searched the bookshelves in the study, she had nothing to read. Presently she dozed off.

It was nearly midnight when Mr van der Beek put down his pen, satisfied with what he had written and desirous of a drink. The sight of Patience asleep, her mouth slightly open, brought him up short in the kitchen doorway. The candle was guttering and he blew it out and put his lamp on the table. As he did so she woke and he put a hand on her arm. 'I am the most thoughtless fool,' he observed, 'and deserve nothing but your scorn. Until we are living normal lives again you will use the study when you have a chance to sit down.'

She had got to her feet. 'Thank you, but that wouldn't do. I might disturb you while you work.'

There was nothing about her, he considered silently, which would disturb him. He said gently, 'Go to bed, Patience. Throw your hot-water bottle down when you get upstairs, I'll bring it up when the kettle has boiled.'

She muttered, 'Goodnight,' hardly awake, wondering sleepily what his fine London friends would say about that. But she threw the bottle down the stairs and he caught it neatly, and when she got back from a rather sketchy bath it was in her bed; there was a mug of hot tea on the bedside table too. She sipped it gratefully, reminding herself that the tea was getting low and she would have to keep it for Miss Murch.

There had been no more snow during the night but there was no sign of a thaw, Miss Murch was better and Mr van der Beek had shovelled his way round to the stables which were used as a garage and listened to the weather forecast on his car radio. The cold spell would last another few days, said a cheerful voice, doubtless from some snug centrally heated retreat; most of East Anglia was without electricity and the telephone, and the voice, even more cheerful, embarked on a list of blocked roads.

Patience counted the candles; there was enough oil for Mr van der Beek's lamp just as long as he didn't sit up until all hours. Coming silently into the kitchen, still obediently in his socks, he found her small person protruding from the store cupboard—she was showing a good deal of leg and he paused to admire them, listening with some amusement to her muffled mutterings. 'Dry lentils—if he'll get me a few carrots we can have soup—I'll have to make some more bread and the flour's almost finished... A tin of prawns; good, there's some rice, I'll make something of those. Mandarins in orange liqueur—they'll be nice. Stem ginger, now that's no use at all; duck mousse with port wine—and canned oysters—I don't know what to do with them; Paxo stuffing—— Oh, I'm so surprised she doesn't make her own.' He watched as she emerged backwards out of the cupboard, still talking. 'He'll have to eat what he's given or go hungry.'

'He'll eat it, don't worry,' said Mr van der Beek and smiled as she spun round like a top. 'Only not the stem ginger, something I have never really relished.'

'How long have you been standing there?'

'I was admiring your legs—they're charming, Patience.'

She stood before him in her dowdy clothes, pushing the hair out of her eyes. She had gone very red but she gave him a steady look.

'Do you always blush when you are paid a compliment?' he wanted to know blandly.

'I don't know.' Despite her red cheeks she spoke matter-of-factly. 'I can't remember being paid one. What was the weather forecast?'

He told her. 'The food's getting low? I'll take the shovel and get to the shed and fetch up some potatoes and onions. I'm sure you can perform clever culinary miracles with them.'

For the next two days there was no snow and almost no wind; a thaw was predicted and not before time. Miss Murch, well enough to spend the day in the kitchen in her dressing-gown and wrapped in a blanket, had nothing good to say about anything, which was unfair, for Patience, well supplied with the potatoes Mr van der Beek had hauled up to the house, a feat requiring some strength—which he had, and unlimited patience, which, strangely enough, he also had—took pains to present that vegetable in a variety of guises and had become adept at making scones and a dough which was almost bread but not quite.

The stores were low indeed when on the following day Mr van der Beek came in from fetching wood to say that there was a snowplough down the lane. Halted for the moment by a deep drift, but rescue was in sight.

'Once they're through, I'll drive you home,' he promised.

'Miss Murch isn't well enough to cope,' Patience pointed out.

'I'll take the Land Rover and ferry Mrs Perch and Mrs Croft to and fro for a few days—you take two or three days off. You deserve them.'

'You'll never get through the lane. Not even in a Land Rover.'

He didn't bother to answer her. It was Miss Murch who spoke. 'You may go to the butcher and the grocer for me, Patience; I will give you a list. You seem to have used almost all my stores.'

'Well, we had to eat,' said Patience weakly.

'We still have to for another day at least,' declared Mr van der Beek. 'Patience has done wonders—I for one have enjoyed every morsel she has offered me.'

'I have been rather poorly,' said Miss Murch with dignity. 'It will be a pleasure to have milk in my tea again.'

Patience caught Mr van der Beek's eye and he gave her a bland look; she imagined he would look like that if one of his patients made some observation of which he didn't approve.

Twenty-four hours later she was perched beside him in the Land Rover, holding her breath as he ploughed his way through the frozen snow, skidding from side to side, getting out with the shovel from time to time to clear a smoother path, not saying a word when they got stuck in a drift and had to reverse. Her only comfort was Basil, perfectly happy since he was with his master, sitting just behind her and licking the back of her neck from time to time.

The main street of the village had been more or less cleared but the snow was piled high everywhere else. Mr van der Beek stopped outside her home and got out, commanding her to stay where she was. The tiny front garden was buried under its white blanket although there was a narrow path made by a variety of footprints. He banged the door knocker and presently the door was opened and Aunt Polly, swathed in a variety of woolly garments, poked her head out.

He greeted her gravely. 'I have brought Patience back,' he told her. 'I hope you haven't been too worried about her; it was quite impossible for her to come down to the village.'

Aunt Polly beamed at him. 'My dear young man, how very relieved we are that she is safe and in good hands. Do come in—she is with you?' She peered round his massive person.

'In the Land Rover. I'll fetch her.'

Patience, impatient to be home, skipped out of the Land Rover and fell flat on her face, to be hauled to her feet and dusted down as though she were an old coat. 'I told you to stay where you were,' he reminded her mildly. 'Do you suppose your aunts will mind if Basil comes in too?'

'No, of course not.' She put a cautious foot on to an icy patch and he caught her by the arm, whistled to Basil and handed her over to her aunt. The three of them, as well as Basil, filled the small hall, and when they were joined by Aunt Bessy Patience took charge, begged Mr van der Beek to take off his sheepskin jacket and urged him into the sitting-room. The fire in the grate was small, but since the room was small too it felt pleasantly warm. Basil threaded his way cautiously towards it and settled himself before it.

'That's Basil,' said Patience, introducing Mr van der Beek.

'Do sit down,' begged Aunt Bessy. 'Such trying weather, is it not? Patience, dear, will you make a pot of tea? Mrs Dodge left some scones and of course we have plenty of milk—the tractor comes down from Slade's Farm each morning and the young people in the village fetch the milk from it and bring it round.'

Mr van der Beek got up when Patience did. 'Patience has been very hardworking during these last few days—my housekeeper has had the flu and we depended on her entirely. I'll carry the tray in.'

There was no gas or electricity but a small oil stove with a kettle already boiling on it. 'Milk in our tea,' murmured Mr van der Beek, taking the tray from her.

She paused as she buttered scones. 'You must take some back with you...'

'Among other things. I have a shopping-list from Miss Murch which will take me the rest of the day to work through. I must go and see Mrs Croft and Mrs Perch too and persuade them to come for an hour or so. You are to stay at home for two days, Patience; I'll fetch you on the third morning. Do not attempt to walk even if there is a thaw by then.'

They went back to the drawing-room and listened to the old ladies chatting about the weather and how old Mr Soames had fallen and broken an arm and some naughty boys had thrown snowballs at Major Thomas's sitting-room windows and broken a pane of glass. Presently they turned their attention upon their guest.

'You are not married, Mr van der Beek?' asked Aunt Bessy.

'Er—no, Miss Martin.'

'A doctor—a surgeon, are you?—should have a wife. It adds stability to his lifestyle. Personally I would never go to a doctor who wasn't a family man.'

Mr van der Beek looked astonished but observed at his smoothest that a married man certainly gave one the feeling of confidence.

'Then you must find yourself a wife, young man,' said Aunt Polly. 'You are nicely settled in at the house? Once the winter is over you will enjoy the garden— the roses in summer are delightful.'

'I shall be gone by then,' he pointed out, and presently took his leave.

The aunts settled down again by the fire. 'It is so nice to have you home, dear,' they told Patience. 'You like the work there? You are not doing menial work, I hope? Is the house being well looked after? The housekeeper must have more than enough to do until Mrs Croft and Mrs Perch can go back.'

Patience assured them that she had almost nothing to do, that the house looked splendid and that the housekeeper was a most efficient woman. 'I'll get the supper, shall I?' she suggested, and wondered what Mr van der Beek would eat that evening. By bedtime she was missing him quite badly. Not that he had been particularly friendly, but he had been surprisingly helpful around the house and now and again very kind. She supposed that once the weather was back to normal and life too he would revert to his coolly distant manner, shut up in the study all day and taking no notice of anyone. He must have found the last few days very trying.

Mr van der Beek had returned to the house with the promise of help from Mrs Croft provided that she was fetched and returned each day; Mrs Perch was, for the time being, unable to leave home until her youngest child had recovered from a sharp attack of bronchitis. He had also visited the butcher and the general stores and, although half the things Miss Murch had demanded weren't to be had, he had a useful supply of bacon and eggs, milk and bread. For a man who spent his days and quite often nights in the operating theatre or on the wards and Out-patients, leaving the mundane things of life for others to see to, he had done rather well. Of course Miss Murch would never forgive him for washing up and shovelling coal; she had been his housekeeper for a number of years and taken care that he had never had to lift a finger when there was someone else to lift one for him. As he unpacked his purchases in the kitchen and offered Basil a marrowbone, he reflected on how much he was enjoying himself. It was much later that evening, after a successful session with the book, that he realised that he missed Patience.

A watery sun shone the next day and a thaw set in, bringing with it burst pipes and water tanks, and flooded fields, but it also enabled the farm tractors to take milk to the main roads where it was collected by bulk containers, and Mrs Croft brought the milk and eggs with her when she came each morning, fetched by Mr van der Beek. She brought bread too but Miss Murch had to go without a great many things she considered were sufficiently good for her em-ployer. It shocked her to see him demolishing plates of bacon and eggs and great slabs of bread and butter.

'Is there no chance of returning to London until the winter is over?' she had asked him, feeling quite faint at the thought of the months ahead.

'None whatever,' he had told her cheerfully. 'This is ideal for my work, but when we do return you shall enjoy a quiet time, for I intend to go over to Holland— I have several lectures lined up there, papers to read and so on, and I have business to attend to at my home there. I shall be gone for some weeks.'

With that she had to be content. The flu had left her disinclined for work even though there was very little of that to do now Mrs Croft was coming each day; none the less, Miss Murch had to admit to herself that she missed Patience; there was no one to answer the phone now that it was connected once again, or to fill the oil-lamps each day, make the beds and do all the small tasks which she herself had never bothered about.

Patience was quite ready when Mr van der Beek called for her. She had enjoyed her two days at home. Mrs Dodge had done her best; the little house was clean and tidy but the old ladies had kept Patience busy, delighted to have her back again, and she had enjoyed going to the village shop and spending some of her wages on the little extras they so enjoyed. As soon as the weather improved, she decided, she would beg a free day from Miss Murch and go to Norwich and buy some make-up and a new skirt and a couple of woollen sweaters to go with it. Now, waiting for him to fetch her, she had on her best skirt, a tweed in dark grey, a white blouse and a cardigan the aunts had given her for Christmas—unfortunately it had been chosen for its usefulness and its pattern, in various shades of grey, was what the shop assistant had assured them was serviceable. Mr van der Beek saw none of this when he arrived for she was already in the Burberry with a scarf tied over her head. Thaw or no thaw, it was still very cold.

She bade the aunts goodbye, reminded them that she would be home again that evening, and climbed into the Land Rover beside Mrs Croft, and Mr van der Beek, after a suitable interval of polite exchanges with the old ladies, got in and drove back to the house. Here he deposited his passengers at the back door and drove on round to the garage with Basil beside him.

By the time he got back to the house Mrs Croft was hoovering the sitting-room and Patience, at Miss Murch's request, was arguing with the coal merchant at East Dereham. He stood at the back of the hall, listening to her soft voice not so much arguing as wearing down whoever was at the other end. He had the time to study the grey outfit and find it dispiriting. Blue, he decided, or that soft silvery green—velvet or fine wool and soft suede boots instead of the sensible low-heeled shoes she was wearing. She put down the receiver and turned round and saw him watching her. She didn't speak but slipped away back to the kitchen where Miss Murch gave her a list of things which needed attention. The laundry van was unable to call; there was a washing-machine in the scullery, and perhaps Patience would be good enough to load it. Miss Murch prided herself on the stock of linen she kept but Mr van der Beek's shirts, although numerous, would shortly come to an end and now that they were living in a civilised way once more—this said with a sniff—there was a shortage of napkins and tablecloths.

So Patience sorted the laundry, laid the table in the kitchen for Miss Murch, Mrs Croft and herself, and a more elaborate tray for Mr van der Beek, and went upstairs to make the bed while the washing-machine did its work.

After their lunch she hung everything on the lines stretching across the scullery and then she opened the windows, letting in the cold dry air. Tomorrow she would do the ironing.

She and Mrs Croft were taken home at four o'clock, bidden to be ready at a quarter to ten in the morning and wished a good day.

'Ever so nice, isn't he?' said Mrs Croft. 'Saves us that nasty old walk along the lane. I reckon I'll be able to go on foot in a couple of days, more's the pity.'

'So shall I. It must annoy him very much having to waste time driving us to and fro when he wants to get on with his writing. After all, that's why he came here.'

The snow was slow in going but the roads, even the smaller lanes, were passable. Mrs Croft and Mrs Perch went to work again at their usual time and Patience did too, which meant that now she almost never set eyes on Mr van der Beek. The house was quiet again; he wasn't to be disturbed on any account, said Miss Murch, and they crept around, polishing and dusting as silently as possible, and Patience took care to answer the phone the moment it rang. It rang less often now and they were almost all calls from hospitals or those who gave their names as 'Dr this' or 'Mr that' and demanded to speak to Mr van der Beek personally. She was surprised to find that he received these calls without complaint. Just once a woman's voice had insisted that she be put through to him, declaring that it was a most urgent matter. Patience, her head full of dire domestic disasters, rang the phone in the study, to be blown off her feet with his blast of rage as he came out of that room to find her.

'Did I not say,' he asked in a cold voice to chill her bones, 'that only urgent calls were to be referred to me? Are you not capable of understanding the word urgent? Did I not, at Mr Bennett's suggestion, hire you for the purpose of deflecting such calls so that my time should not be wasted? Have I not——?'

'Just a minute.' Patience's voice was small but clear; she sounded like a kindergarten teacher calling the children to order. 'There is no point in working yourself into a bad temper,' she pointed out in a reasonable voice. 'If you are able to tell me how I am to know the difference between urgent and urgent then I will have no need to pass on calls you don't want. You told me that all calls which were urgent were to be taken by you, and this—this lady said it was an urgent matter. It could have been your wife, your children, your mother, your—your girlfriend.'

He stared down his nose at her. 'You must not let your imagination run away with you, Miss Martin. I have no wife, no children to the best of my knowledge, and my family live in Holland.'

She looked at him calmly. 'I didn't know that, did I?' She gave him a forgiving smile. 'Never mind. I'll try not to do it again.' And then she allowed her thoughts to trip off her tongue. 'Haven't you got a girlfriend?'

He stared at her for a long moment. 'You are an impertinent young woman,' he told her, and laughed quite nastily, and then turned on his heel and went back into the study.

She didn't see him for the rest of the day and went home quite sure that she would be told that her services would no longer be required.

CHAPTER FOUR

MISS MURCH met Patience in the morning with the news that Mr van der Beek had driven himself off to London. 'He's much sought after,' she said importantly. 'He has a splendid reputation in the profession.' It was plain that there was only one profession worth mentioning in Miss Murch's eyes. 'You are to sort through his mail and if there is anything urgent you are to telephone him. He has left the number on his desk. It is a good opportunity to clean the study; you had better do it, Patience. I need not warn you to take great care not to disarrange anything on his desk.' She sniffed. 'And do give the hearth a good polish. I really don't know what the world is coming to with Mr van der Beek insisting on lighting his own fire each morning. I cannot wait for our return to London. Oh, the sooner the better.'

Patience sorted the post; quite a few letters were addressed to Julius—a nice name, she considered, and it suited Mr van der Beek. They were written in another language—she supposed it to be Dutch. She laid them on one side and didn't open the envelopes with 'Private and Confidential' written upon them and heavily underlined. The girlfriend? He might even now be with her. Patience, sorting the bills, allowed her imagination to take over. The girl would be tall and willowy, strikingly good-looking with flashing dark eyes and dark hair to go with them. She was mulling over her clothes when Miss Murch put her head round the door to ask if she was going to be all day. 'I want that study cleaned and polished before you go home,' she insisted.

The room looked nice by the time Patience had finished with it. She had laid the fire in the burnished fireplace, polished the furniture and hoovered every inch of the floor, and then skipped into the garden and picked some more of the forsythia, perked up again once the snow had gone, and arranged it in a vase on the table by the window. She had wasted time peering at the papers on his desk too, feeling sorry for whoever would have to decipher his awful writing and render it fit for the publisher's eye. In any case, even if she could have read it, she was sure she wouldn't understand any of it. The papers were arranged very untidily and she longed to straighten them into neat piles, but probably he liked to work in a muddle. She had read somewhere that very clever people were hopelessly disorganised and she supposed that he was very clever. She sat down at the desk and wondered about him. He had a home in London presumably, but what about his family and real friends? And did he sit in elegant consulting-rooms all day dispensing wisdom about people's insides? Or did he pace the hospital wards with a horde of lesser fry behind him, the way doctors did in films?

Unfortunately for her, he was doing none of these things. The faint sound of the door opening roused her from her daydreaming and the sight of him standing there sent her on to her feet.

'And what might you be doing here?' he asked in a silky voice she didn't much care for. 'Do not tell me that you are cleaning the room because you aren't—you are sitting at my desk, probably poking your nose into my papers, idling away the time in which you should be working for me.'

He came into the room, not hurrying, which somehow made him rather more alarming, but Patience, over her surprise, faced him calmly enough.

'I've cleaned your room and not touched anything and I sat down for a moment to catch my breath, that's all.' Being an honest girl she added, 'I looked at some of the papers but I haven't touched them and, anyway, I couldn't understand a word. If you had come back when you said you would—tomorrow— you would have found the room just as you had left it and been none the wiser.'

He said mildly, 'Your grammar is rather sketchy, isn't it? But I get your meaning. Where is Miss Murch?'

'Oh, she came in here a little while ago to say that she was going down to the village—a taxi came for her.'

'A taxi just to go to the village?'

'It's not dry underfoot yet.'

'And Mrs Perch and Mrs Croft?'

'Oh, they went with her—a bit early but they'd finished. I'm to stay until Miss Murch gets back.'

'And when will that be?'

'Well, she didn't say exactly, but they went about half-past three and I said that I didn't mind if I didn't go exactly at four o'clock...'

'It is well past half-past four. Have you had your tea?'

'I have it when I get home, with the aunts. Shall I make a pot for you?'

'If you please, and when you have done that you may go home. I shall be here when Miss Murch returns.'

She collected her dusters and polish and the hoover and went to put on the kettle and presently went back to the study. It was empty, so she put the tray on the table by the window, put a match to the fire and went to get into her outdoor things. There was no sign of Mr van der Beek. She let herself out of the side-door and as she reached the corner of the house the Bentley nosed to a halt where the path joined the sweep before the house.

Mr van der Beek opened the door. 'Get in,' he invited in what she described to herself as his ordering voice.

'Your tea,' she reminded him.

'If you will get into the car I shall be back here within five minutes.'

So she got in. Outside the little terraced house she said, 'Will you explain to Miss Murch, please? She expected me to stay—and thank you for the lift.'

He bade her good evening gravely and drove away. The aunts, watching from the sitting-room window, chided her gently for not inviting him in.

Two weeks went by and January gave way reluctantly to February. There was no more snow but plenty of wind and rain and occasionally a heavy frost. Patience, tramping to and fro in her wellies, sniffed the air and even decided that there was the merest hint of spring in the air. She was kept busy enough during her day's work, and, to give Miss Murch her due, the house ran on oiled wheels; Mr van der Beek had wanted complete quiet and she made sure that he had it. Patience glimpsed him from time to time, leaving the house with Basil for his early morning walk, or crossing the hall on the way to the study, but beyond a brief greeting he rarely spoke to her. She dealt with his post, made her neat lists and coped with the answering of most of his letters, and in between whiles kept the vases filled with catkins, Christmas roses and chrysanthemums, flourishing in the greenhouse once more now that old Ned was looking after them. Despite Miss Murch's constant demands for a greater variety of vegetables, he doggedly persisted in nurturing daffodils and tulips, which had been neglected since the aunts had left the house. In a week or so he would allow Patience to cut some of them for the house; in the meantime she foraged around the lanes and banks for the first primroses and snowdrops, setting small bowls of them around the rooms, even sneaking into the study and leaving primroses on the table, just where the thin sunlight would highlight them. Mr van der Beek had paused to look at them and the next morning he had scrawled, 'I like the primroses; please keep the bowl filled!' on top of his laconic directions as to what she was to do with the post.

It was a week later that he thrust open the study door as she was crossing the hall. 'Patience—come here and help me clear up this mess.' And when she followed him in, he said, 'I opened the window and a gust of wind blew almost everything on to the floor—heaven alone knows what a muddle it has made of my papers.'

'Well, I dare say it isn't as bad as it looks,' said Patience soothingly, and she got down on her hands and knees and started piling the sheets one by one into tidy bundles. 'If I do this you can go through each bundle and sort out the pages. They are numbered?'

'Yes, of course they are. This is going to take all day...'

'A couple of hours. You really ought to get all this lot typed.'

'And have still another of you here? I wanted peace and quiet...'

'You get it, Mr van der Beek. You are left undisturbed for hours on end and it isn't very nice of you to say that when we creep round the house all day, hardly daring to sneeze.'

He let out a crack of laughter. 'No one would think to look at you...' He didn't finish but presently said, 'So I'm to get a typist?' He was at his desk sorting rapidly. 'Who would you suggest; yourself perhaps?'

She ignored the smooth sarcasm. 'But I'm already working here as a general factotum, aren't I?'

'You can type?'

'Yes.' She didn't look up from the rapidly diminishing chaos.

'I suppose you can do shorthand as well?'

'Well, yes, actually I can. I'm a little out of practice. I took a course when I left school; the aunts thought that I should be occupied doing something useful. We had a housekeeper then, you see.'

For anyone else he would have felt pity at the dullness of her life but Patience, he was quite certain, neither needed pity, nor expected it.

'I shall arrange for a typewriter and you may try your hand at deciphering my writing and transforming it into something my publisher can read.'

'I'm not sure that I can read your writing...'

'At least let us give it a try. If you feel you can cope that will be splendid and then you shall become my personal assistant.'

'Thank you, Mr van der Beek, but who is to do my work around the house?'

He said carelessly, 'Oh, we will get extra help from the village. You will continue to answer the telephone and parley with the tradespeople and so on. You will of course be paid a suitable salary. Let me see . . .' He mentioned a sum which widened her lovely eyes.

'Goodness me, that's far too much.'

'It is, I believe, the going rate for typists and office workers. You may telephone any large agency and check that if you wish.'

'No, no, of course I won't—that is, I'm sure you're right, Mr van der Beek.'

She handed him the last of the pages and got up. 'I'd like to try, please, but if I'm not good enough you will tell me, won't you?'

Mr van der Beek, who had never put up with second best either in his home or his work, assured her that he would.

It was another two days before she saw him again; he called her into the study soon after she arrived one morning, wished her a civil good morning and told her to choose which typewriter she preferred.

There were three on the table, one of them an electronic model, the other two the latest in streamlined efficiency. She examined them all, taking her time and choosing the latter. 'I'm not used to an electronic typewriter,' she explained. 'I believe they're very easy and quick, but I'd have to waste time getting to know it.' She pointed to her choice. 'I'd like that one, please.' She added, 'I'd like to work in the dining-room if you don't mind; the phone's there and it's near the door if anyone comes and Miss Murch wants me to answer.'

He shrugged. 'Just as you please. Take this first chapter and see how you get on.'

Several times during the next few hours she almost gave up in despair. It wasn't only his writing; she was baffled by words she had never heard of—indeed very little of the first few pages made sense to her at all. She offered them that afternoon, feeling doubtful about the outcome, bracing herself against his cool criticism. He read her efforts through without comment before remarking in the mildest of voices, 'Quite satisfactory. See to the post when you get here tomorrow and let me have the list and then get on with the typing. Have you all you need? I told them to send everything you were likely to want with the machine...'

'I've everything, thank you.'

'Good. Good day to you, Patience.' His head was bent over the papers on his desk; he had forgotten her, she supposed, his mind already engrossed in his writing.

She said, 'Good evening,' on a gentle breath and slipped out of the room without a sound. He hadn't heard her go but he knew she wasn't there any more; he found that disquieting.

A quiet country girl with a sharp tongue at times and an abominable taste in clothes; there was no reason at all why he should be aware of her. He went back to his writing and forgot her.

Patience went back to the poky little house and told her aunts the news. They nodded their elderly heads.

'Most suitable work, dear,' said Aunt Bessy. 'You say he has offered you a larger salary?'

She told them that too and then spent some time explaining that what seemed a small fortune was in fact an adequate salary since money values had changed a good deal in the last year or two. This was an argument they had never quite understood—a pound note to them had been sufficient to purchase food for several days instead of a small metal coin just about enough to buy a lamb chop or four oranges. They had known that they had lost most of their money but they had never grasped what a difference it was going to make to their lives and Patience had done her best to conceal that from them; they had lived a good deal in the past and she saw no reason to worry them unncessarily. Certainly the extra money would be more than welcome... They accepted the change in their fortunes with equanimity, merely remarking that dear Patience must buy herself some pretty clothes.

Patience had had the same idea; she had seen the looks Mr van der Beek had cast at her from time to time—indifference mingled with pity—and she had found them hard to bear. It would be nice to see the look of admiration appear on his handsome features. Her face might be an unassuming one but she had a nice figure and legs... She spent a pleasant few minutes before she went to sleep that night planning an outfit.

She worked hard the next few weeks, patiently retyping her inevitable mistakes and his drastic alterations, fitting in the phone calls and acting as go-between with Miss Murch and the local shopkeepers, for Miss Murch had the unhappy knack of rubbing them up the wrong way, unmindful of the fact that in their eyes she was a foreigner. It was when she had had her third week's increased wages that she asked if she might have a day off.

Mr van der Beek, his splendid nose buried in a ponderous volume, didn't bother to lift his head. 'Why?'

A number of replies were on the tip of her tongue; she swallowed them all. 'Well, I haven't had one yet,' she pointed out reasonably, 'and I want to go to Norwich.' Before he could ask why again, she added, 'To go shopping.'

He looked up then, studying her person, clad sensibly in the tweed skirt and a blouse under a cardigan. 'In that case go by all means. Have you sufficient money?'

It was on the tip of her tongue to say that no woman ever had sufficient money when she went shopping. She thanked him politely, and asked, 'When?'

'When you've retyped this chapter that I'm correcting. You have made some imaginative attempts at the medical terms, most of them incorrect.'

'I'd get them right if you wrote more clearly,' she pointed out in a reasonable voice and then, goaded by the unfairness of it, added, 'If you operate as untidily as you write, I'm sorry for your patients.'

His look was scathing; so was his voice. 'You have far too sharp a tongue, Miss Martin, and not for the first time. You will probably turn into a shrew and lead your husband the devil of a life.' He handed her the pages he had corrected. 'Now go away and make sense of these.' He picked up his pen without looking at her again.

She had no intention of apologising, but she did take care to return his work quite faultlessly typed this time.

She went to Norwich several days later, much to Miss Murch's disapproval, leaving the aunts in Mrs Dodge's care for the day. It was the tail-end of winter now and the dress shops were showing spring outfits. She studied the chic boutiques, knowing that their prices were away above her head but getting from them a good idea of what was fashionable, and then she made her way to Marks and Spencer and the bigger High Street stores.

She hadn't a great deal of money to spend; she laid it out on a pleated skirt, fuchsia and blue on a French navy background, and topped it with a short blue jacket, then she searched for and found a fuchsia blouse which looked like silk and wasn't. She also found a cotton-knit top in navy blue, and then, rummaging through the bargain rail, found a caramel and cream jersey dress, very plain but a splendid fit. There wasn't much money left, so she searched for shoes— navy blue courts with a nice little heel. They were cheap and wouldn't last long but they went with everything she had bought. She had a cup of coffee and a sandwich, bought two pretty silk shawls for the aunts, and caught the bus home.

It was a great pity that it poured with rain for the next two days so that there was no chance of wearing her new clothes, but on the third morning the sun shone and, although it was cold, it wasn't so cold that she couldn't wear the new jacket and skirt. She carried the shoes—they would never stand up to the muddy lane—but once at the house she hung up the new jacket carefully and in the knitted top and skirt sat down behind her typewriter. Miss Murch had greeted her grudgingly, remarking that she had been spending her money; it remained for Mr van der Beek to notice her changed appearance.

Halfway through the morning he opened the study door and called to her to go in. She took what she had typed and went in quietly, bidding him good morning. His glance was brief and wholly uninterested. 'I shall have to go up to London,' he told her, 'nothing to do with the book—go on with as much as you can, will you? I shall be away for a few days; I'm not sure how many at the moment. There should be enough to keep you busy.'

She bent to pat Basil's head. 'Very well, Mr van der Beek. Is there anything else which you would like me to do while you are away?'

'I think not, thank you, Patience. Take these, will you, and get on with them? I'm not leaving until this evening, so come in here in the morning and collect whatever is on the desk.' His cool gaze swept over her. 'Thank you.'

Back at the typewriter, Patience had a hard job convincing herself that it didn't matter in the least that he hadn't even noticed her outfit. She told herself stoutly that she had bought the clothes to please herself and with no other thought in mind. A palpable lie she had no intention of admitting to.

She was covering her machine ready to go home when he came out of the study again. 'It occurs to me that if you have time on your hands you might get started on the reference pages. I've roughed them out; see what you can make of them.' At the door he turned round. 'I like the new clothes, Patience,' he told her. 'Did you think that I hadn't noticed?' He smiled kindly.

She was an honest girl. 'Well, yes, but it wouldn't have mattered—I mean I bought them because I wanted to look nice and they were pretty.'

'You look very nice,' he assured her gravely, and went away again.

She went to the study the next morning, and, since he wasn't there and was not likely to be for a few days, tidied his desk quite ruthlessly. Just as he had said, he had left plenty of work for her: pages of his terrible writing, unnumbered to make things harder, and a great many little notes on scraps of paper. Obviously he had had sudden flashes of inspiration, jotted them down and forgotten all about them. It was a good thing that he was going to be away for several days.

She finished tidying the desk and found an envelope addressed to herself wedged into a scribbling pad. It contained her wages, not due until the end of the week—so he wouldn't be back before the weekend; he might appear to work in fearful disorder, she reflected, but there was nothing disorderly about his mind. She burrowed some more and came up with a thin bundle of cheques with a note attached; she was to pay the butcher and the general stores in the village and post a cheque to the coal merchant and the plumber who had dealt with the damage the snow had caused. She went to her typewriter then although she didn't start work immediately but sat thinking. She hoped that he wasn't going to be away for too long; the house seemed strangely empty when he wasn't there.

It was more than a week before he returned and long before then she had to admit to herself that she missed him—him and his cold eyes, his bland remoteness and his sudden kindnesses and his indifference.

Mr van der Beek, prowling round Theatre half an hour before he was to operate upon a patient who badly needed a new valve in his heart, showed, for the moment, none of these qualities. He was whistling cheerfully and thinking about Patience. He had been thinking about her a good deal and laughing at himself for doing so. He told himself that there was nothing about her to attract his thoughts; a small dab of a girl, although he had to admit that she had beautiful eyes, clear and trusting as a small girl's. But she had been full of surprises; no one, seeing her for the first time, would credit her with the sound common sense she undoubtedly possessed. Besides, she could cook even when there had been nothing to cook with. The people in the village liked her—he suspected that they would do anything reasonable she might ask of them—and she had courage. To keep two old ladies, used to living in comfort, happy in that poky house on limited means needed courage. She deserved better things from life. The right clothes would help. Mr van der Beek didn't know much about women's clothes, but he had quite definite ideas about what would suit Patience—for a start he would throw out every grey or brown garment in her meagre wardrobe...

He was prevented from further speculation by Theatre Sister, a female dragon with a waspish tongue and a heart of gold, reminding him that his patient was on the way up from the ward.

The operation was lengthy and he didn't leave the hospital until he knew that his patient in Intensive Care was making satisfactory progress. It was early evening as he drove himself away from the vast sprawling hospital in the heart of the city and by the time he reached his home it was almost dark. The house was one of an old row of beautifully maintained houses facing the river at Chiswick. It being the end house, it had the advantage of a double garage in the alley behind the terrace and he drove the car straight in before going into the house to be met by a middle-aged man with a bald head and a round merry face.

He wished Mr van der Beek good evening with the reserved friendliness of an old servant who knew his place. 'There's a nice fire in the drawing-room,' he pointed out. 'Dinner'll be half an hour, if that suits you, sir?'

'Thank you, Dobbs.' Mr van der Beek picked up his letters from the Hepplewhite side-table and made for his drawing-room, Basil at his heels.

'Miss Murch telephoned, sir,' said Dobbs, and his master turned to look at him; Dobbs was Miss Murch's ardent admirer. 'Just to make sure that everything was going smoothly.'

'I hope you reassured her. Is all well in Norfolk?'

'I understand that everything is satisfactory there, sir.'

Dobbs went soft-footedly away to cast an eye over the housemaid, who had taken over Miss Murch's duties while she was away, leaving Mr van der Beek to sit in his great chair by the fire with Basil on his feet and the unopened letters on his knee. The room was a charming one, furnished with a nicely balanced mixture of comfortable chairs and sofas and several pieces of walnut and yew-wood from the mid-eighteenth century. There was a magnificent bracket clock of walnut and gilded brass and on either side of it a bookcase and a secretaire, both superb examples of Dutch marquetry. The walls were panelled and painted white and hung with fine paintings. The curtains were of deep rich bronze brocade, a colour echoed in the rugs strewn upon the floor. Mr van der Beek allowed his gaze to roam around the room before opening the first of his letters and the unbidden thought flashed through his mind that he would like to see Patience's reaction to it.

He opened the next letter, frowning. He was allowing his thoughts to wander too much in the girl's direction. It was perhaps a good thing that the phone rang before he could think too much about that; his senior registrar, not quite satisfied with the condition of the patient they had operated upon earlier that day. Mr van der Bleek listened carefully, sighed soundlessly and said that he would be on his way in five minutes.

Dobbs, about to serve the soup, tut-tutted softly but made no comment. What would have been the use anyway? Mr van der Beek had always put his work first; the soup would not spoil and the housemaid could put the dessert back in the fridge. He himself would prepare the sole *véronique* the moment Mr van der Beek got back home. Heaven alone knew when that would be, thought Dobbs gloomily. He brightened a little, though, as his master went to the door.

'Ring Miss Murch, will you, please, Dobbs? Tell her I intend going up to Norfolk in two days' time. Make sure that everything is OK there, will you?'

It was after ten o'clock by the time he got back
home, his patient once more on the road to recovery.
He ate his meal, thanked Dobbs and the maid for
their trouble, and took himself and Basil off for a
brisk walk before going to bed. There were several
ideas seething in his head concerning his book but he
had had a long day. Letting himself into his quiet
house, he found himself wondering if Patience was
already in bed and asleep . . .

She was in bed but she wasn't asleep; she was sitting
up, doing sums on the back of an envelope. Even after
she had bolstered the aunts' income to a decent level,
allowed for the rainy day and paid Mrs Dodge, there
was a little money over. Not a great deal, but enough
for her to augment her new wardrobe. A dress, she
had decided, something patterned that would look
right during most of the year, but before that the aunts
needed new hats. They seldom went out but church
on Sunday was a must and they had never condoned
a bare head in church. Getting them to Norwich would
be a bit of an undertaking but there were no hat shops
nearer. She would have to wait a few weeks before
she asked for another day off and she had wondered
if, now that she was working almost all day for Mr
van der Beek, she might suggest that she had a day
in the week free instead of Sunday. Miss Murch
wouldn't approve of that, but then she disapproved
of so many things. She wondered briefly what Mr van
der Beek was doing, conjuring up an erroneous picture
of him in a dinner-jacket, escorting some lovely girl
to one of London's nightclubs. That he was hardly
nightclub material hadn't occurred to her; she had
only the vaguest idea of his work and that mainly
gleaned from the TV where handsome surgeons in

theatre green strode out of the operating theatre looking noble. Not that he looked noble; mostly he looked aloof and faintly annoyed.

She put down the envelope and curled up in her bed; even when he was annoyed or just being his usual austere self she rather liked him.

Mr van der Beek, at the end of a busy day at the outpatients clinic, his private patients dealt with and his operation cases doing well, decided to return to Themelswick earlier than he had intended and when Dobbs asked if he should let Miss Murch know he was told to do nothing, 'For I shall probably stop off in Norwich—I've friends there and they'll put me up for the night. There's a call I promised to make at the hospital there—the professor of general surgery there is a friend of mine.'

He changed his mind when he was approaching Norwich and, as it was already early evening, he decided he could just as easily drive over one morning. He took the road to Themelswick and on to the house. Patience would be gone, he reflected, but he could look over whatever she had typed before getting on with his writing.

He went up the short drive slowly, surprised that there was only one window lighted. The dining-room. He drove round to the garage and went in through the unlocked garden door. There was no one in the kitchen; he went through to the hall and stopped short at the sound of the typewriter. It was after six o'clock and Patience had no reason to be there. He crossed the hall and opened the dining-room door.

Patience looked up, made a small bleating sound and went pale with fright. But indignation took over.

'How dare you frighten me like that?' She spoke with a regrettable squeak. 'You could have been anyone...'

He ignored this silly remark. 'I'm sorry if I startled you. Where is Miss Murch?'

'There's a church bazaar in the village.' She glanced at the clock. 'She won't be long now.'

'You're alone in the house?'

'Yes.'

'Were you aware that the garden door is unlocked?'

'Well, yes. Miss Murch said she'd come in that way; the front door's bolted and barred for the night.'

'You are not nervous?'

'Not really—you see this was my home for years.'

He nodded. 'Of course, I was forgetting, but be so good in future to keep the doors locked if you should be here on your own.' He saw then that the fire had died down. 'Are you not cold?'

'Well, a bit, but I wear these.' She held out her small nicely kept hands encased in knitted gloves. Smiling at him, she added, 'They are very cosy.'

There was only a bright reading lamp on the table, by its light he could see that she was wearing the blue plaid design skirt and the fuchsia blouse; here and there her hair had come a little loose too and now that she had got her colour back she looked almost pretty. He said casually, 'How has the work gone?'

'Quite well, I hope. I've finished what you left and started on the index. I don't suppose you did any writing while you were in London?'

'None at all. Will your aunts not be worried by your absence?'

'Mrs Perch said she would go and tell them I would be a little late.'

'In that case might we have a cup of tea together and glance through the work you have done?'

He turned to go out of the room. 'I'll be in the study—there is a fire there, I presume?'

'No. I'm afraid not. No one goes in there when you are away, only me with your papers.'

'I, not me,' he corrected her blandly. 'Then I'll bring everything here while you boil the kettle.'

By the time she got back with the tea-tray and a tin of biscuits he was sitting on the other side of the table, turning over the pile of typed pages. He got up as she went in, took the tray from her and carried their cups and saucers over to the table. 'You have done a great deal of work,' he observed. 'I'll go through it tonight; you can get on with the index until I've something for you to type.'

It seemed too good a chance to miss. 'If there's not too much work for a day or two could I please have another day off? You see I can't do any shopping on a Sunday. I know I've plenty of time when I go home each afternoon to go to the stores and Mr Crouch, but I mean *shopping* . . .'

'Clothes. Yes, of course you may have a day off. Tomorrow, if you like. I should have something for you by the following day. You're going to Norwich?'

She nodded and passed him the biscuits. 'Thank you. I won't need to go again for a long time, only the aunts must have new hats . . .'

'Naturally,' agreed Mr van der Beek, keeping a straight face. Very much to his surprise he heard himself telling her that he had just remembered that he had an appointment with a friend at Norwich Hospital on the following morning. 'If your aunts would like it, I should be delighted to give you all a

lift. Unfortunately I won't be able to bring you back.'
Last-minute caution made him say that. Just because
the girl looked small and lonely and he had frightened
her without meaning to, there was no reason to hand
out favours...

She thanked him matter-of-factly, just as Miss
Murch came back, very put out because Mr van der
Beek had arrived and she hadn't been there to welcome
him. 'Oh, don't mind about that,' he told her very
cheerfully. 'Patience did that.'

CHAPTER FIVE

MR VAN DER BEEK fetched the car and drove Patience to the village and went indoors with her to speak to the aunts and renew his offer of a lift. They were delighted, both at the idea of new hats and a ride in his car, and kept him talking for several minutes until he excused himself and left, reflecting that he must have been mad to have suggested it in the first place. His ordered life seemed to be disintegrating day by day. He would get the book finished—he was well ahead in any case—and go back to London to the work he loved and look up his friends, perhaps even think seriously of marrying...

'A charming man,' declared Aunt Bessy, 'such good manners and so kind and thoughtful. I dare say he is a splendid doctor.'

'He's a surgeon, Aunt Bessy.'

'All more or less the same thing,' said Aunt Bessy largely. 'Now, my dear, what type of hats shall we purchase? Something suitable for the entire year—a good felt, perhaps?'

They discussed millinery for the rest of the evening and it was bedtime before Patience had a chance to wonder if Mr van der Beek was regretting his offer. He had said that he intended writing...

He appeared to have no regrets when he came to fetch them the following morning, and, since Aunt Bessy indicated graciously that she would sit beside him so that they might talk, Patience found herself

with Aunt Polly in the back with Basil panting happily
at their feet.

Aunt Bessy, having decided that she liked Mr van
der Beek, proceeded to cross-examine him as to his
work, his family and his life. This she did with a gentle
persistence and perfect manners but she had met her
match; he answered her readily enough and told her
nothing. Patience, listening from the back seat to her
aunt's high penetrating voice, wished herself anywhere but where she was. She wasn't helped by Aunt
Polly either, who every now and then put in her own
gentle oar.

Once in Norwich, he drove down King Street,
turned into one of the smaller streets close to the
Cathedral and asked where they would like to be put
down.

'This will do very well, thank you,' said Patience
quickly. 'I hope we haven't taken you out of your
way. I expect you are going to the Norfolk and
Norwich Hospital, you'll have to go through Rose
Lane and All Saints' and then into Queen's Road—
there's an awful lot of one-way traffic.'

He agreed politely that there was and something in
his dry tone made her feel foolish. The hateful man
probably knew Norwich better than she did.

As he helped the old ladies out of the car he asked
how they would get back. 'There's a bus this
afternoon—most convenient—and it stops in the
village quite near our house. Thank you very much
for driving us in; it was most kind of you.' She looked
up at him, looming over them and found him smiling
and, for some reason, and to her vexation, she blushed
again.

He got back into the car, invited Basil to sit beside him and sat watching the three of them walk away. Patience in the middle, holding an arm of each of her aunts, upright and dignified and frail in their old-fashioned clothes.

The aunts always bought their hats at one shop and nowhere else. It hadn't occurred to them that they could have chosen exactly what they wanted at any one of the High Street stores at a fraction of the cost. Patience sat watching them try on a number of hats, taking their time, arguing gently as to the merits of dark brown or black, but in the end they were satisfied and she led them from the shop with the new hats, considerably the poorer.

They had a light lunch then she sat them on a seat in the Close and flew off to the shops again, promising to be back within half an hour or so. With an eye to the warmer days she bought a dress in a pretty floral print with a tie neckline and long sleeves; it was in a mixture of wool and cotton and she judged that she would be able to wear it for a good part of the year. There was enough money over for stockings and cosmetics; she bought a lipstick which the sales lady assured her did wonders for the face and a nourishing cream which would do wonders for wrinkles. She had none yet, but at any moment one might appear...

She went back to the old ladies sitting happily in the Close, enjoying the thin sunshine, and led them away to a café for tea before they caught the bus back home. Public transport was rather a let-down after the Bentley but the aunts never complained; they sat, content with their day's outing, surrounded by children going home from school and busy mothers laden with plastic shopping bags, talking happily

about the future when they would return to their old
home. They had taken it for granted that once Mr van
der Beek had left they would be able to go back to
the house and Patience hadn't the heart to disabuse
them.

After the severe winter, spring was making a brave
start. Provided that she wore the chunky cardigan that
she had knitted for herself during the winter, the
caramel and cream dress was warm enough and once
she reached the house the cardigan could be dis-
carded, for Mr van der Beek saw to it that his house
was adequately heated. It had been worth the slightly
chilly walk too for he had observed carelessly as she
was handing in the day's work that the dress became
her. At the risk of catching cold, she wore it for the
rest of that week.

Mr van der Beek was writing furiously now, as
though it was imperative that he should finish as soon
as possible. If he intended to return to London as
soon as the book had been delivered to the publisher
then another six weeks would see him gone. Patience
began to worry about that—he had signed an
agreement for six months, Mr Bennett had told her,
but, if he wanted to leave before then, would he still
have to pay for the full period? And she would be
without work. She wrote and asked Mr Bennett about
it and was relieved to be told that Mr van der Beek
had undertaken to pay six months' rent whether he
stayed for the whole of that time or not. A relief,
though she still admitted to herself that she was just
as worried about not seeing him any more.

She worked as hard as usual, though, managing to
find time to arrange daffodils and tulips around the
house, give Miss Murch a hand and smooth the

somewhat thorny relationship between that lady and the village shop; Mr Crouch had never recovered from her scathing comments on his pork chops, and the village stores, not having got around to the kind of cash register which did everything, quite often made mistakes, especially when the shop was full and the little sums jotted down on a handy piece of paper got mislaid. The mistakes were put right, but Miss Murch's opinion of grocer's shops which weren't within a stone's throw of Harrods was low. No one in the village liked her over-much, although Patience suspected that the housekeeper felt out of her depth and that once back in what she called civilisation she would turn into quite a nice woman. Certainly she was loyal to Mr van der Beek and ran his household on oiled wheels.

It was more than a week after the trip to Norwich that Patience, watching Mr van der Beek, his hands in his pockets and with Basil beside him, strolling around the garden, answered the phone beside her.

The man on the other end sounded urgent and asked to speak to Mr van der Beek without delay.

'I'll have to fetch him from the garden—who shall I say you are?'

'His registrar, and please be quick.'

She could hear Basil barking joyfully as she ran from the garden door and saw the pair of them almost at the kitchen garden. 'Hi!' screamed Patience at the top of her lungs. 'Come back—there is an urgent call for you!' As he turned and started towards her, she added, 'He says he's a registrar.'

He had reached her, swept her back indoors with him and was at the phone before she had crossed the hall, and since there was nowhere else for her to go she went into the kitchen, where Miss Murch told her that if she had nothing better to do she might put the milk on for the coffee.

She had the saucepan in her hand when he came into the kitchen. He took no notice of her but spoke to Miss Murch. 'I'm leaving for London now. No, no, I don't want coffee. You know where to get me if I'm needed.'

He turned to Patience as he went out of the room. 'There's work on the desk,' he told her. 'If I'm not back, get on with the indexing.'

She followed him out. 'Very well,' and then she asked, 'Is it something very urgent?'

'A heart transplant. Now run along and don't ask so many questions.'

A most unfair remark. She watched him drive away from her window but he didn't look at the house as he went by.

She wished that she could have gone with him, seen for herself this other side of his life about which she knew less than nothing. An important part of his life, she guessed, more important even than this book he was so engrossed in. Then there was his private life—where did he live? she wondered. He wasn't married but he must have friends, perhaps a woman he loved... She sat idle, feeling sad.

He had said get on with the indexing and once she had finished typing what he had written she got on with that, a slow, painstaking task but she had got through quite a lot of it by the time he came back again three days later.

She knew he was back because she heard Basil barking but there was no sign of him until just before she was ready to leave that afternoon. He came into the dining-room with a handful of bits of paper. 'Notes,' he told her, 'will you get them sorted? Let me have them before you go, please, I want to use them this evening.'

Before he went away he asked, 'Everything all right?'

Her, 'Yes, thank you, Mr van der Beek,' was quiet. She would have liked to have asked if the heart transplant had been a success but she could see that, judging from the remote expression on his face, she wouldn't get an answer, anyway.

It was long past four o'clock by the time she had sorted out the notes but he didn't seem to notice that when she took them to the study, wished him good evening and took herself off to the aunts.

Typing up his manuscript was taking up more and more of her time; she took her morning coffee to the sound of Miss Murch's gentle grumbling. 'I was told that you would take some of the routine tasks off my hands but it seems that it is not so.' She gave Patience a look suggestive that it was all her fault.

'Mr van der Beek has got someone else from the village,' she pointed out, 'and I still deal with the tradespeople and answer the telephone.' She added, greatly daring, 'Have you talked to him about it?'

Miss Murch looked affronted. 'It is not my place to question my employer...'

'Well,' said Patience, reasonably, 'I don't see that anything can be done about it, then, do you?'

Miss Murch gave her a nasty look. 'I only hope that this book is quickly finished and we can return to London.'

Patience didn't answer, for she hoped exactly the opposite.

Spring had come at last and the country was green and alive once more. Patience began to ponder over her summer wardrobe. There was money in the bank now; not much but a small nest egg against the rainy day which loomed ever threatening on her horizon. All the same, there was enough to buy a cotton dress or two both for herself and the aunts. Another day off would have to be asked for.

She decided to wait for the right moment, and that required patience, for Mr van der Beek was being more remote than usual—polite but in an absent-minded manner which made it difficult to ask for favours—but when he handed her a sheaf of papers, remarking that they were the last chapter, she knew that she would have to ask soon. There were almost two months of the six left and he would certainly go back to London now that the book was finished. There was still the index to type, of course, and her fears were lessened when he observed that he would be getting the proofs not long after the last chapter had been handed in. 'Two or three weeks' work,' he told her. 'A pity you won't be able to help me with it. Miss Murch will be delighted to have you back again to do the flowers . . .'

She made no comment. Did he really think that was all she did around the house? Men, thought Patience, however clever, could be extremely unobservant.

Two days later she took her finished work to the study, tapped on the door and went in to find him on the phone.

He glanced up and the look on his face puzzled her; relief, with a kind of wry amusement too. He spoke into the phone and asked, to surprise her, 'Do you believe that prayers are answered, Patience?'

It seemed a strange question, but she answered at once, 'Of course.'

'Good—so do I.' He spoke again into the telephone and rang off. 'Sit down; I have a favour to ask of you.'

She put the papers on his desk and sat down with Basil's head on her knee. Then, since Mr van der Beek remained silent, she said kindly, 'Is it something awkward? I'll be glad to help if I can.' A sudden thought struck her. 'Do you want me to leave now that the book is done? I'm sure it's difficult giving someone the sack, but it's quite all right—I've been expecting it sooner or later.'

Mr van der Beek leaned back in his chair, looking at her with some amusement. 'How you do ramble on,' he observed. 'I'm touched at your concern for my feelings, but you're barking up the wrong tree. I have no intention of giving you the sack, as you so elegantly put it; indeed, on the contrary, I should like you to undertake a temporary job for me, or rather for my sister.'

'Your sister?'

'Don't, I beg you, repeat everything I say like a poll parrot, just sit still and listen.'

'I'm listening and I'm sitting still,' said Patience snappily, 'and stop talking as though you were addressing a meeting...'

His eyebrows rose at that, and then he laughed. No one had talked to him like that for a long time and he rather enjoyed it. 'I will be brief. My sister and her husband and small daughter are staying at my house in Chiswick. They brought their nanny with them but she has just been admitted to hospital with appendicitis and my sister has phoned to ask how and where she can get a temporary nanny. Don't run away with the idea that she isn't capable of looking after the child herself; she is expecting another baby in a couple of months and needs another pair of hands. I fancy yours would do very nicely.'

'You want me to go to London and look after a little child? It's kind of you to think of me, Mr van der Beek, but I'm not a nanny and what am I going to do with the aunts?'

'You're a sensible young woman and I believe you like children. As for the aunts, would they consent to spending a week or two here with Miss Murch, who I'm sure will be delighted to have their company...?'

'Yes, well—they're not used to doing anything around the house; they never have done you see and now they are too old...'

The stare he turned on her should have shrivelled her up. 'My dear Patience, we are perhaps at cross purposes. I am proposing that your aunts should stay here as my guests; Miss Murch will look after them as such and they will lack for nothing. You can be easy on that score.'

'Oh, sorry. It's kind of you to think of that...'

'I'm not being kind, I am arranging this to suit my sister and myself! I shall be driving to London tomorrow afternoon and I hope that you will agree to come with me.'

'For how long?'

'Two weeks. My sister will be going back to Holland then, and Nanny should be back before that although not able to do much. In any case, arrangements can be made in Holland. That is not my concern.' He smiled at her with such charm that her heart danced against her ribs. 'Please do come, Patience.'

'Yes. All right, provided that the aunts are happy about it. Does Miss Murch know?'

'Not yet. It wasn't until you came into the room just now that I saw what could be done. You had better go home and talk to the aunts; bring them here directly after lunch tomorrow.' He frowned. 'No, better still, I'll fetch you, you can have half an hour to settle them in before we leave. It's rather short notice... I'll phone the garage and arrange for a taxi to be available should they wish to go back home to the house in the village to fetch something.' He added, 'And church, of course. I'll talk to Miss Murch; you can safely leave everything to me.'

Patience nodded; she was sure of that.

The aunts were not to be hurried into instant agreement, although Patience could see that they liked the idea. They had never said so but she was aware that they disliked the little house they now lived in and longed for the comfort and spaciousness of their old home. They agreed, presently, making it sound as though they were conferring a favour upon Mr van der Beek and pronouncing themselves satisfied that the work she was to do in London was quite suitable. The discussion having been brought to a satisfactory conclusion, she set about packing their cases and, that done, seived through her own wardrobe, seeking the best of what she had, folding it away neatly into the old-fashioned leather suitcase which had been her mother's. It was as heavy as lead, but well polished, and it had class.

They were called for promptly by a suave Mr van der Beek, driven to the house, and the aunts handed over to Miss Murch, who received them with proper deference, led them away to their old bedrooms and offered to unpack for them. Mr van der Beek had obviously given his instructions, thought Patience; she fancied that her aunts were going to live in great comfort for the next two weeks. She spent a little time with them, bade them goodbye, exchanged civilities with Miss Murch and got into the car once more, her luggage in the boot and Basil on the back seat.

'It's a two-hour drive,' observed Mr van der Beek laconically and didn't speak again for a long time. He drove down through Ipswich and Colchester and on to Chelmsford and, the journey three parts done, stopped in a small village just south of that town. 'Tea?' he asked. 'There's a nice little place here where they make delicious buttered toast.'

Patience's mouth watered; lunch seemed a very long time ago and it had been a scanty one and she longed for a cup of tea. He urged her inside to a table by the window and said matter-of-factly, 'Off you go. I'll order, shall I?'

She went; she had been rehearsing several suitable sentences to utter, feeling shy, but he hadn't needed even a hint. Of course, he had a sister...

When she got back the teapot was on the table and a covered dish, housing, she hoped, the buttered toast. He got up as she reached him and pulled out her chair. 'Mind Basil, he's hiding underneath.'

'Oh, do they mind him being here?'

'No one minds Basil. He's had a bowl of water and a biscuit already.' He smiled across the little table at her; she really looked quite pretty in the caramel and cream dress and she was delightfully restful; Marijke would like her. Making up for his long silence on the journey, he embarked on a gentle conversation about nothing much until they were ready to leave.

It was the rush-hour in London by the time they reached that city. Mr van der Beek picked his way through the traffic, nipping up and down obscure streets, confusing Patience, who had a scant knowledge of the place anyway, but always driving west until they reached Chiswick and the quiet surroundings of his home.

Patience, being helped out of the car, clutched his arm. 'Look,' she told him, 'there's the river—what a wonderful spot. You wouldn't know that it was London, would you?' She turned to look at the house. 'Is it really yours?'

He gave her an amused glance. 'Yes, it is. Why? Are you surprised?'

She shook her head. 'No, not really, it's right for you, isn't it? It's just that I have always thought of you living in one of those modern flats with balconies and a man at the door.'

'Heaven forbid. I'm flattered that you have spared me a thought, Patience.'

She blushed, wishing she could say something witty in reply, but he didn't seem to notice her awkwardness, urging her across the pavement to where the house door stood open. Dobbs was there, beaming a welcome, silently agreeing with Miss Murch's opinion that Patience was a nice young lady, a bit old-fashioned but that didn't matter; nor did it matter she had no looks worth mentioning. He had been warned by her to keep a fatherly eye on Patience, something he was prepared to do in any case since it would please Miss Murch.

He admitted them to the house, bowed politely over the hand held out to him by Patience, and informed them that Mevrouw ter Katte was in the sitting-room with the little girl. He needed to raise his voice to tell them this for the childish voice, raised in furious screams, made normal speech impossible.

Mr van der Beek turned to Patience. 'You see how necessary it is to have you here to restore peace to my house? We have arrived not a moment too soon.'

The infantile bellows increased. 'Perhaps if we were to say hello?'

With Dobbs preceding them they crossed the hall and went into a room at the back of the house. It was not a large room but it was very comfortably furnished and sitting in one of the wing chairs was Mr van der Beek's sister: a fair-haired girl with a beautiful face and eyes of a very bright blue. Her hair was curly and cut short and at the moment very untidy. She gave a small scream when she saw them. 'Julius—you've come...' She broke into Dutch and then switched back to English. 'Sorry; I was so pleased to see Julius—you must be Patience. I am so grateful to you—Rosie's being a handful...'

She lifted her face for her brother's kiss and held out a hand to Patience. 'Usually I can cope but I'm feeling a bit—how do you say?—off colour.'

Mr van der Beek had swung his niece off his sister's lap and sat her in the crook of his arm. 'Where's Rinus?'

'He's gone for a walk.'

'The coward. You're tired, *lieveling*. Shall we throw this tiresome young lady into her bed and have a quiet talk about ways and means? How is Nanny?'

'She's got a secondary infection.' Mevrouw ter Katte looked at Patience. 'Do you suppose that you could manage just for a week or two?'

'Oh, yes,' said Patience. She had lost her heart to the tear-stained cherub leaning against her uncle's shoulder. 'Though you will have to tell me how you like things done. If she will come with me now I'll undress her and bath her and get her into bed.'

'You don't know where everything is,' the cherub's mother said wistfully.

'I'll take Rosie upstairs and show Patience round at the same time. You stay here and have a drink ready for us when we come down; we shall need it.'

Rosie had stopped bawling and her doleful sniffs had given way to giggles as she was borne up the gracefully curved staircase at the back of the hall. The house was larger than it appeared to be from the outside; the square landing had several doors leading from it and there was a narrow passage towards the back of the house. Mr van der Beek opened a door at the end of it to disclose a pretty little room over-looking a good-sized garden behind the house. 'You will be next door,' he told Patience, 'in Nanny's room. The bathroom is on the other side.'

He sat down on the side of the small bed with Rosie on his knee. 'If you get a bath ready we'll dunk her and pop her into bed.'

Patience looked doubtfully at him. 'I could manage,' she began.

'I know—but a little help won't come amiss on your first day here. She's a friendly child but only if she likes you.'

Fate was kind. Rosie consented to be undressed by Patience, was bathed, robed in a nightgown and popped into her bed while her uncle sat in the small easy-chair by the window. Once she was tucked up, he kissed her goodnight, observed that she would be asleep in five minutes and then went away.

Well, really, thought Patience crossly, Now what am I supposed to do once Rosie is asleep?

However, Rosie wasn't quite ready to sleep yet. 'Sing,' she demanded in a small voice.

So Patience sang, dredging up memories of nursery rhymes and working her way through all those she could remember and then, since she had come to an end, embarking on 'My old man's a dustman.'

Mr van der Beek, coming back upstairs to see how she was faring, stood listening to her clear gentle voice and choked back a laugh. She finished the verse and, since there was silence now, he went in. 'Asleep?'

When she nodded he said, 'Good, sorry to throw you in at the deep end like this but we arrived at the right moment and it was best to take advantage of it. Dobbs told the housemaid—her name's Jenny—to unpack your things, so please come down as soon as you've tidied yourself.'

He bent over the bed for a moment and then went away and Patience went to her own room, which was a little larger than Rosie's and charming with its pastel colours and the pretty lampshades. She did her face and her hair, took another look at Rosie and went downstairs. Dobbs was in the hall.

'In here, miss,' he begged, and opened the drawing-room door. Mr van der Beek was there and so was his sister and her husband, a big thickset man with pale hair and a pleasant rugged face.

The men got up. 'Patience, this is Rinus ter Katte,' and, when they had shaken hands, 'Sit down, do, and have a drink. After dinner we must have a talk.'

Patience was enchanted with the room and presently when they crossed the hall to the dining-room she found it equally beautiful; William and Mary, she guessed, with some handsome marquetry. The table, covered in a damask cloth, was set with heavy silver and fine china and the glasses were old—she knew that because there were two just like them in Aunt Bessy's corner cupboard—baluster wine glasses, eighteenth-century and valuable. Aunt Bessy always said that they would pay for her funeral and that of Aunt Polly and were on no account to be sold for any other purpose, but here they were in everyday use...

Patience was hungry; she did full justice to the tiny onion tarts, the tarragon chicken accompanied by creamed potatoes and a variety of vegetables followed by an apple tart and cream and finally cheese and biscuits. All the while Mevrouw ter Katte talked, sometimes in Dutch, excusing herself first. 'For I am rusty in my English—it is good that you are here, Patience, for I can practise with you.' She beamed across the table, her pretty face friendly.

'Now we will go and sit by the fire and explain everything to you.'

When they were sitting over their coffee presently, she began, 'This is how it was arranged with Nanny but if you do not like it you say so, yes?'

She didn't wait for an answer. 'Do not think that I leave Rosie always with her nurse. That is not so but I have not been well, you understand. I become tired easily and that is not good for the baby. I will have Rosie after breakfast for one hour or so and then

I will like to go out with my husband, perhaps to lunch, to shop... if you will care for her until—after tea perhaps? We will have her then for an hour or so before you put her to bed. Is that agreeable to you?' She looked anxious. 'You will have very little time for yourself and you must think that I am a selfish woman, but indeed I am not.'

'I think it will do you a great deal of good to go out and shop and enjoy yourself,' said Patience, 'and you're not selfish. I'm sure Rosie will be great fun; I only hope that I'll be a good nanny.' She hesitated. 'Your own nanny doesn't mind?'

'She is glad that there is someone to help me. I have been to see her today and she expressed relief. It is most unfortunate that she is ill.'

The two men hadn't said a word and presently Mr van der Beek took himself off to sit in his study, wishing Patience goodnight as he went. 'I shall be at the hospital all day tomorrow and won't see you until the evening,' he observed as he went.

It had been a long day; Patience took herself off to bed, first peeping into the room next door to make sure that Rosie slept. Her bed had been turned down, the curtains drawn, her nightie laid on the pillow, a bottle of spring water and a glass arranged on a little tray on the bedside table. Very welcoming. She had a leisurely bath and got into bed, mindful of the fact that small children woke early.

Rosie was no exception; Patience wakened to find Rosie crouching beside her, prodding her with small gentle fingers. Neither spoke much of the other's language but they managed very nicely and presently Patience got up, sat Rosie in the middle of the bed while she dressed and then dressed her and crept through the quiet house down to the kitchen and out into the garden behind the house. It was chilly, but a bright morning, and they capered around on the smooth lawn behind the flowerbeds, and Mr van der Beek, preparing to take himself and Basil for a quick walk before breakfast, wasted a good deal of time watching them from the window. He heard them creeping indoors again while he was at the table but made no attempt to see them; for one thing he had no time to spare and for another he had promised himself that he would see as little of Patience as possible—the girl was becoming an obsession, something he would not allow in his ordered life.

She and Rosie breakfasted in a little room which she supposed was a kind of day nursery. It was cosily furnished with a nice big table, a magnificent rocking horse and a dolls' house which Rosie was still too small to appreciate although Patience couldn't wait to open its doors.

They breakfasted happily enough. Jenny bore a laden tray upstairs and Rosie, secure in her high chair, fed herself after a fashion. She was a charming child and well-behaved for the most part. Patience cleaned her up after their meal and bore her down to the dining-room where her mother and father were finishing their breakfast.

Mevrouw ter Katte looked rested. 'All is well?' she wanted to know. 'Now we shall play with Rosie and you will please be free for an hour. If you will come for her at half-past ten? Julius said that if you wish you should walk along the river and take the air.'

So Patience put on a jacket and walked briskly, enjoying the sight of the river. It was surprisingly quiet; she supposed that the shops and main streets lay somewhere behind the house. Tomorrow she might explore a bit but for today she was content just to look around her. It was all very different from Themelswick—no wonder Miss Murch had had such difficulty in settling down. She couldn't think why Mr van der Beek needed to leave such a lovely spot in order to obtain peace and quiet, but perhaps he had a great many friends and a busy social life. Perhaps, too, she would learn something of that while she was in the house.

Rosie was quite happy to go with her when she got back to the house; there was a small public garden close by, Dobbs told her, and she could take Rosie there in her pushchair. 'Her nanny takes a ball and they play for half an hour or so. Rosie has her dinner about midday—unless you wish otherwise I will serve your lunch at the same time, miss, then you will have a little time to yourself while Rosie has her nap.'

The day went well and the moppet was happy enough with Patience, gabbling away in her mother tongue, listening with every appearance of understanding to Patience's replies in plain English. Midday dinner, an unknown hazard, went off smoothly. Patience ate her own light meal at the same time and settled Rosie for her nap. She slept at once and Patience cast around for something to do while she slept. She would have liked a book to read but she didn't like to go downstairs and look for one; she didn't know where to look anyway. There was a window overlooking the garden at the end of the passage where their rooms were; she opened it and hung out, admiring its well-planned spaciousness.

'He must have a great deal of money.' She spoke out loud for there was no one around and a voice, any voice, even her own, would be welcome. 'He's a lucky man.'

'Indeed he is,' said Mr van der Beek, so close to her that when she bounced round, breathless with sudden fright, she found her face in his waistcoat.

'You really must not do that,' she hissed at him. 'I might have screamed and wakened Rosie.'

'Once she is asleep the Royal Marines Band could play in her room and she wouldn't stir.' He smiled down at her. 'Are you lonely?'

'No, no. How could one be lonely with Rosie? It's just a bit strange.'

He hadn't intended to come home before the evening but he was glad that he had now; she looked forlorn despite her matter-of-fact manner, although why should he concern himself about her...?

CHAPTER SIX

Mr van der Beek had no intention of searching his feelings too deeply; he told himself that he was concerned about Patience because he had uprooted her so ruthlessly from her quiet village life and it behoved him to make sure that she had settled down.

He stood beside her, looking out of the window at his well tended garden. He said casually, 'I'm free on Saturday; I shall be driving into Berkshire with Marijke and Rinus and Rosie to lunch with friends. We shan't be back until four o'clock or thereabouts. A good idea if you take the morning off once you've fed Rosie and handed her over. I dare say you would like to do some shopping. I'll tell Dobbs to have lunch ready for you around one o'clock if you would like that?'

'Thank you, yes, I would.' Her eyes sparkled; at Marks and Spencer and Selfridges and their like, she was bound to find a couple of summer dresses within her budget. Mr van der Beek, watching her face, reminded himself to leave her wages on the breakfast table and suppressed a sudden urge to whisk her away to one or other of the exquisite boutiques in and round Bond Street.

He moved away. 'That's settled, then.' He sounded remote, 'Let me know if there is anything which worries you.'

She didn't see him for the rest of the week, only at dinner each evening, when he was careful to include her in the conversation with cool good manners. She thought about it in the fastness of her bedroom, getting ready for bed. She supposed that he found it awkward to have to entertain her while his sister and brother-in-law were there, but then, she argued logically, if they weren't there she wouldn't be either. Anyway, she had been urged to stand in for Nanny and she was doing her best to be unobtrusive.

Being unobtrusive wasn't enough; Mr van der Beek was as aware of her as if he had been sitting in a room knowing that there was a mouse in the corner, not making a sound but all the same leaving him in no doubt as to its presence.

Patience, with a week's wages tucked into her pocket, watched them drive off on the Saturday morning. She was enjoying looking after Rosie but she had to admit that almost a whole day to herself would be nice. The only cloud on the horizon was Mr van der Beek's manner towards her: cool, almost cold, meticulously polite too, so that she became tongue-tied and avoided him as much as possible, and that, she reflected, wasn't difficult.

Armed with the numbers of the buses she would need to take, information offered by an attentive Dobbs, she made herself ready and set out for the shops—it was still fairly early. At the top of Oxford Street she got off the bus and made for Marks and Spencer at Marble Arch and, after one careful inspection, decided that she didn't need to go anywhere else. Very much later she found herself in Oxford Street again, the pleased owner of a cotton jersey dress in a dashing pink, a flowered skirt, and several tops to go with it; there had been enough money to buy undies, too, and a useful little rainproof jacket.

Happily laden, she had coffee in a nearby café and caught a bus back to Chiswick.

Dobbs cast a fatherly eye over her as he admitted her. 'A successful morning, miss?' he enquired. 'You must be ready for your lunch. I've everything prepared when you would like to have it. In the sitting-room at the back of the house.'

He served her a little bowl of piping hot onion soup, a mushroom omelette which melted in her mouth, a salad of chicory and apple and a *crème brulée* by way of pudding. As he poured her coffee he said, 'Mr van der Beek asked me to suggest that you might like to telephone your aunts while the house is quiet. There is a telephone in the hall or in the drawing-room, miss.'

He withdrew silently and presently she went into the drawing-room and dialled the well remembered number. Miss Murch answered her, her normally severe manner positively friendly. She enquired quite kindly about Patience, expressed the hope that she was enjoying herself, and went to fetch the aunts.

The old ladies had never liked the telephone and their conversation was brief. However, they were happy, she could hear that, and they were being very well looked after. She put down the receiver and wandered out into the hall, uncertain as to whether she should go to her room or sit in the room which was being used as a nursery. Her problem was solved for her by Dobbs, who appeared discreetly beside her and said, 'I have arranged the newspapers and a few magazines in the drawing-room; I dare say you will be glad of an hour sitting quietly. Mr van der Beek telephoned to say that they would not be back until after five o'clock. I will serve you tea at four o'clock if that suits you?'

So she spent a blissful afternoon, reading, dozing and presently eating the tiny cucumber sandwiches and little cakes which Dobbs brought. Even the tea tasted better, poured from a small silver teapot.

She heard the car an hour later and Dobbs went to admit the ter Kattes and Rosie. Mevrouw ter Katte looked tired and pale, and Patience took Rosie from her at once while Mijnheer ter Katte took his wife upstairs.

Rosie was pleased to see her; she sat on her lap, having her miniature cardigan removed and talking nineteen to the dozen. 'Now isn't that lovely?' declared Patience in answer to all the unintelligible gabble. 'Tell me what you've been doing all day.'

Not understanding each other made no difference; they held an animated conversation with a good deal of giggling and neither of them heard Mr van der Beek come into the room. He stood by the door, watching them, smiling a little. Patience, in her floral-patterned dress, listening with great attention to her small companion, looked exactly right sitting there in his drawing-room. He thought of the elegant young woman who had been staying with their friends and who had done her best to attract him all day. She had been witty and amusing, very pretty and exquisitely dressed, but then she had taken no trouble with Rosie beyond a first cursory 'hello', and here was Patience, her cheap little dress being creased and scuffed by Rosie and paying no heed to it despite the fact that, as far as he could see, she could ill afford to have it spoilt. He frowned; he wasted too much time thinking about the girl.

His, 'Good evening, Patience,' was uttered with the polite coolness she had come to expect from him, but it didn't dim the pleasure in her face at the sight of him.

She answered him quietly. 'I'll take Rosie upstairs for her bath and give her supper; she must be quite tired.' She picked up the moppet. 'Say good night to your uncle, Rosie,' and, when the child had lifted a cheek for his kiss, whisked her off upstairs. Mr van der Beek, used, without conceit, to the eagerness of the opposite sex to bear him company, felt intrigued. Patience was avoiding him, an altogether different matter from his avoidance of her. He went and sat in his chair with Basil beside him; it would be interesting to see if he could change that...

Rosie kept her fully occupied until it was time for dinner. She changed into the floral skirt and one of the pretty tops, piled her hair with severity and went downstairs to the drawing-room. Mevrouw ter Katte, fully recovered, was sitting with her husband on one of the sofas and Mr van der Beek was in his chair. He got up as she went in to get her a drink and Mevrouw ter Katte said, 'Do come and sit here, near me, Patience. Have you had a nice day? And is Rosie quite all right?'

'She's fine. Asleep already, and she ate up all her supper. Do you feel rested, Mevrouw ter Katte?'

'Yes, thank you. It is such a relief that Rosie is fond of you. She became tired, though; our friends have children also and she became excited. It was nice to see them again, though.' She looked across at her brother. 'They do not change, Julius, do they? And such a lovely house. Did you like Sadie Beauchamp? She is pretty and charming—great that you got on well together.'

'Yes, we did.' He spoke deliberately, his eyes on Patience, sitting silent, her quiet hands clasped on her flowered lap.

'She is of course too clever for me,' remarked his sister, 'I am not clever in that way, but I have been clever enough to have my beautiful Rosie.' She smiled around her, secure in her husband's love and her brother's affection, and everyone laughed. They were halfway through dinner when Mr van der Beek was called away, reappearing briefly to say that he didn't know when he would be back, and left the house, and shortly after they had had their coffee Patience said goodnight and went to her room. Rosie would be awake early.

She was awake long before morning, though, sitting up in her little bed in the small hours, bawling her childish fears from some probably frightening dream. Patience, half strangled by Rosie's small arms, took her from the blankets and walked up and down soothing her, wishing she could understand what the child was saying, talking to her in a soothing voice and begging her to stop crying. Rosie was bent on telling her all about it in a voice sodden with tears, interrupted by the occasional bellow.

'Oh, hush, my love,' said Patience, 'you'll wake everyone up. Mummy and Daddy and Uncle Julius...'

'Uncle Julius hasn't got to his bed yet,' he said as he came into the room, took Rosie from her and sat down on the little bed. He was still fully dressed and he was tired and Patience, looking at the weary lines in his face, had the sudden feeling that all that mattered was to erase those same lines, tell him to go to bed while she got him a warm drink and saw that he had a good night's sleep. If he had a wife, she thought, she would do that for him, and at the same time she was almost swept away with the strong desire to be that wife. She stood looking at him whispering to Rosie, struck dumb by her discovery, her eyes wide and her mouth half open. He said, hardly looking at her, which was just as well, 'She has had a bad dream; she'll be all right now that she has told me about it—too much excitement today, I expect. She is already half asleep.'

He settled Rosie back into her bed and stood a minute, watching Patience tuck her in and then draw up a chair. 'Sing,' commanded Rosie in a sleepy voice.

'Yes, sing, Patience. She'll be asleep in a few minutes. Goodnight.' He sounded even more austere than usual.

Bad dreams or no, Rosie was awake at her usual time. Patience dressed her and then herself and carried her downstairs. It was a lovely morning; they would have a drink in the kitchen and then go into the garden for a little while. She was crossing the hall when Mr van der Beek came out of his study and made for the front door. He looked elegant, but he always did, and wore the face of a man who had had a good night's sleep. As he went past her he wished her a brisk good morning.

'You're never going to work!' exclaimed Patience. 'You've only been in bed for a few hours and you were up half the night; you can't burn the candle at both ends.'

The astonished amusement on his face stopped her. She went red, feeling quite sick at what she might have gone on to say. She almost choked at the thought; she had forgotten everything—all that mattered was that she loved him and he needed looking after. Now the horror of what she had said sent the colour from her cheeks. 'Oh, dear,' said Patience, with deep feeling.

Mr van der Beek was eyeing her narrowly, but he said nothing, only came back from the door, kissed Rosie's cheek and then, very deliberately, kissed Patience on the mouth. He went away without uttering a word.

Patience spent the rest of the day trying to think of a way to avoid him when he returned home in the evening—a great waste of time, for he didn't come; instead his sister told Patience at teatime that he had been sent for urgently to go to Northern Ireland to operate on a soldier who had a bullet within a millimetre of his heart. 'And I only hope that no one shoots him while he's there,' observed Marijke gloomily.

It was two days before she saw him again and by then it was almost the end of her second week, and moreover Nanny would be leaving hospital very shortly. There would be nothing for it but to return to Themelswick, collect the aunts and go back to the little terraced house, for certainly there would be no more work for her. Mr van der Beek would leave the house, so would Miss Murch, and there would be all the miserable business of trying to sell it again. True, she had saved most of her wages and there was enough money to eke out her aunts' pensions for a few months. She pondered the matter as she attended to Rosie's small wants and took her for a brisk walk with the pushchair. She had barely glimpsed Mr van der Beek that morning and his sister and her husband had gone to the hospital to see Nanny. They had been gone a long time and she wondered what they were doing.

They were sitting on either side of Nanny's easy-chair in her hospital room and Mr van der Beek was lounging on the bed.

'I think the best thing would be for you——' he nodded at his brother-in-law '—to drive Nanny back home, say in a couple of days, see her settled in with her sister for a week or two or until she feels fit enough to take up her duties once more. Marijke can stay here until I'm free—a day or so at the most—and I'll drive her, Patience and Rosie back to Holland with me. Patience can stay with you until Nanny is quite fit again.'

'Yes, but perhaps Patience won't want to come...'

Mr van der Beek looked bland. 'Oh, I think she will. I'll take her out, give her a meal somewhere and explain. She knows her aunts are safe at Themelswick and she needs the money. I should think that you, Nanny, will be quite fit a fortnight or three weeks from now.'

They had been speaking in Dutch; now he got to his feet as a nurse came into the room and said in English, 'I'd like a word with whoever is on duty, Nurse. Is the registrar available?'

He wandered off with her and returned presently to say, 'Well, that's settled.' He glanced at his watch. 'I must go back to the hospital, but I'll be home in a couple of hours. I'll take Patience out this evening and explain things to her.'

Patience had handed Rosie over to her mother and was sitting in the room used as the nursery, having tea. She had kicked off her shoes and was devouring the sandwiches and cakes Dobbs had brought while she scanned the day's news from the newspaper he had thoughtfully brought with him. Mr van der Beek's voice, coldly disapproving, caused her to choke on a crumb so that he had to thump her on the back until she had quietened down.

'What I said was, why are you having your tea here? Tea is served in the drawing-room. You are not a servant, Patience.'

She drew a whooping breath. 'No, I know that. Rosie is with her mother in the drawing-room and she very kindly suggested that I might like an hour to myself before I put Rosie to bed. That's why I'm here.' She added kindly, 'You shouldn't jump to conclusions so hastily.'

He was looking at her so strangely that she said quickly, 'It's very kind of you to bother, though.'

'When you have put Rosie to bed, I should like to take you out, Patience.' Her sudden delight at this remark was quenched at once when he went on, 'There is something I have to discuss with you.'

Patience might be in love but she had plenty of common sense. 'If you are going to tell me that you don't need me any more you can do it now if you like. I've been expecting it; Nanny must be almost well again.'

'Kindly do as I ask, Patience. We will leave the house at half-past seven. Do not allow your suppositions to override your good sense.'

Left to herself once more, Patience poured the last of the tea and drank it thoughtfully. She had seldom been invited out to dine but this wasn't an invitation, it was a foregone conclusion, at least on his part. For two pins she wouldn't go, knowing even as she thought it that of course she would go. He wasn't in the least bit interested in her but at least she would be in his company for an hour or two and it would be an occasion to treasure later on. She put down her teacup and fell to wondering what she should wear.

It would have to be the caramel and cream dress, not exactly 'after six' wear but it was elegant and well made and quite obviously not from the high street stores. She couldn't bear the thought of embarrassing him by being dressed all wrong; the flowered dress was pretty, so were the tops and the skirt, but anyone could see where they had come from.

He took her to a small, well known restaurant in Walton Street—Ma Cuisine—where, despite its high reputation and smart clientele, he guessed that her modest wardrobe would give her no cause to feel awkward. For his part she could have worn a sack, but he was aware that she was sensitive about her appearance and the last thing he wanted to do was make her unhappy, even the least bit uneasy.

Patience, looking around her as they sat down, sighed with relief; the women around them were smartly dressed but there were no sequinned tops or eye-catching satiny outfits and the men, like Mr van der Beek, wore beautifully tailored suits and the kind of tie which cost as much as her cotton dress, perhaps more. She smiled shyly at Mr van der Beek, who was watching her under drooping lids, and said, 'This is very nice.'

He knew exactly what she meant; he hadn't failed to see the sigh of relief and the swift female appraisal of the women there. He said easily, 'It is quiet and the food is good. Shall we have a drink while we order?'

The food was indeed delicious; *mousseline* of lobster with a champagne sauce, spring lamb with a faintly garlicky sauce and a *nougat glacé* with raspberries to finish, and all the while Mr van der Beek kept the conversation light and impersonal, smiling faintly at Patience's attempts to find out why he wanted to talk to her. It was as she poured their coffee and accepted a *petit four* from the dish he offered her that he said, 'You have been a great help to Marijke, Patience; she—we are most grateful. You have had almost no time to yourself and we appreciate that, but now there is more... We have been to see Nanny and I've talked to her surgeon who has been looking after her. She is well enough to go back to Holland but not fit to return to her duties for another few weeks. Would you consider returning with Marijke and Rosie until she is able to work again? A question of three weeks at the outside. I shall be delighted if your aunts would agree to stay at the house at Themelswick while you are away, Miss Murch will continue to look after them and Marijke will pay you the same salary as you are receiving now.' He paused, but when she opened her mouth to speak he said, 'No, don't say anything for the moment. When we go back think about it and perhaps telephone your aunts in the morning and see if they agree. I have no wish to coerce you.'

She longed to tell him that she needed no coercion. It was like being offered the fairy on top of the Christmas tree. There was something she had to know, however. 'Will you be in Holland too?' she asked.

'Yes. For most of the time. I have one or two things lined up... I think it might be best if Rinus goes back with Nanny and settles her with her sister; I'll drive over as soon as I'm free and take you and Marijke and Rosie with me.'

'Basil?'

He smiled a little. 'He has to stay with Dobbs. I spend more time here than in Holland at the moment. He's fond of Dobbs.'

She remembered something and asked, 'Whereabouts in Holland?'

'Rinus lives in den Haag so you would be there.'

'You live there too?'

'No, but Holland is a small country and I live near by.'

Near by could be anywhere. She sensed a gentle snub and lifted her chin. 'When would you want me to go?'

'Rinus intends taking Nanny back in two days' time. Supposing I drive you up to Themelswick so that you can talk to your aunts and collect anything you may want to take with you? I have to go to Norwich so if we leave early you can have the day and I'll collect you in the early evening.'

Everything had been planned, she could see that now—he had been very sure of her, but then he must know that she needed the money. She had been, she reflected bitterly, of great convenience to him; first his house and his book and now his niece. It was a great pity that she loved him so much that she would have cheerfully agreed to do anything he asked of her.

She said now in her sensible way, 'I expect it will be all right. I'm sure the aunts won't mind when I explain, and it isn't as though you were a stranger.'

He agreed gravely, hiding amusement. He had never met anyone quite like her before. His mother would have called her an old-fashioned girl, but she was sturdily independent and sensible. She was also, at times, remarkably tart. He said now, 'I'll drive you up the day after tomorrow while Rinus is still here to give a hand with Rosie. We will leave very early—about eight o'clock...'

'Very well.'

'Now that is settled, shall we have another pot of coffee?'

He had nothing more to say about the journey to Holland and after due thought she decided not to ask; she might only get another polite snub. Instead they discussed the books they had read, discovering that their tastes were similar; indeed, they agreed upon so many things, reflected Patience, that in other circumstances they might have been really good friends. They were, of course, behaving in a most civil fashion towards each other, but she sensed that there was more to her companion than he was allowing her to see. Possibly he was making an effort to be agreeable so that he could be sure she would agree to go to Holland with Rosie. No sooner thought than said. 'You need not have taken me out, you know,' she assured him. 'I mean I didn't need buttering up so that I would agree to take Nanny's place. You must know that I need a job...'

She looked across the table at him and sat back rather suddenly in her chair. He hadn't moved but the sudden blaze of anger in his face struck her like a blow. 'Shall we consider that last remark unsaid?' he asked softly.

She made herself look at him. 'I'm sorry, I shouldn't have said that—at least, I put it badly, didn't I?'

'Very badly. Don't ever talk like that again, Patience.'

'No, I won't. I hope I haven't spoilt the evening. I—I've had a lovely time.'

The anger had gone—he was smiling. Perhaps she had imagined the ferocity of it. 'While you are in Holland you must try and see something of the country. I'm sure that if you ask Marijke you will be able to save up your free time and stay on for a few days after Nanny returns. There is a great deal of interest...' He began to talk about the lesser-known delights of his country.

It was late when they got back but Dobbs was still up, ready to offer coffee or drinks. Patience said her goodnights, reiterated her thanks for her dinner, hugged Basil and went up to her room. She glanced back at the top of the stairs; Mr van der Beek was already going out again with Basil. She smiled at his vast back; she would see him again in the morning.

Rosie was awake early; Patience got dressed, dressed the moppet and bore her downstairs. Dobbs met them in the hall with a cheerful good morning and the offer of a cup of tea for Patience and a glass of milk for Rosie.

'Mr van der Beek left just after four o'clock,' he told her. 'Another of those heart transplants. He won't be home for the rest of the day.'

It had been nearly midnight when they had got back last night; he wouldn't have had more than three hours' sleep. 'He works too hard,' said Patience worriedly, and Dobbs agreed, thinking to himself that his boss couldn't do better than marry such a nice young lady—she wouldn't stop him from doing his work, he thought shrewdly, but she'd see that life was made as easy for him as possible. Of course he himself, and dear Miss Murch, did their best, but the boss never listened to them—he'd have to listen to a wife...

He didn't come home all day, and he still wasn't home when she put Rosie to bed, changed her dress and went downstairs to the drawing-room. The ter Kattes were there and Rinus got up at once to get her a drink. They had been shopping, and Marijke said, 'I don't know what we should have done without you, Patience; we've been able to do all the things we had planned thanks to you. I do hope you'll be happy with us in den Haag. You will be able to have much more time to yourself there; we have a marvellous housekeeper and a maid who adores Rosie, so you will have a free time each day—there is so much to see.'

They began to talk about their home and den Haag and presently, since Mr van der Beek wasn't back, they went in to dinner. The meal was over and they were back in the drawing-room when the phone by his chair rang. Rinus answered it; he spoke in Dutch so that Patience knew that it was Mr van der Beek on the other end. She was steeling herself to the disappointment of not going to Themelswick in the morning when he put down the telephone.

'Julius—he's staying at the hospital for a while yet. He did a heart transplant early today and wants to keep an eye on the patient. Patience, he says he will expect you to be ready to leave here by half-past eight in the morning. I'll let Dobbs know and he'll arrange breakfast for you...'

Relief flooded through her person but she sounded her usual matter-of-fact self. 'I'll get Rosie up and dressed before I go. She could have her breakfast with me and I'll hand her over at the very last minute.'

'Thank you. I'll collect her—I expect you'll have breakfast in the nursery. Anyway, Dobbs will arrange everything and let you know.'

Patience went to her room soon after that to put everything ready for the morning. Dobbs had been waiting for her in the hall. She would be called in good time, he told her; breakfast would be served in the room used as a nursery and she need not worry about anything. He sounded very soothing; it was pleasant to have someone to plan for her, when she had become used to doing that for herself and the aunts.

She was awakened by Jenny with a cup of tea and the information that breakfast would be on the table by a quarter to eight and, since Rosie for once was still asleep, she got up and dressed—the caramel and cream dress again, well made enough to stand up to the busy day she saw ahead of her. She did her hair with some severity, made sure that everything was to hand and went to wake Rosie.

They had just finished their breakfast when she heard the house door shut and Basil's cheerful bark, and a few minutes later Mijnheer ter Katte, true to his word, came to carry off his small daughter.

'Have a pleasant day,' he said. 'You will be glad to see your aunts again. Julius came back in the small hours, had his breakfast some time ago and went out with Basil. Are you ready? Can we do anything to help?'

'I'm quite ready,' Patience said, and kissed Rosie's round cheek. 'I hope you don't have too busy a day.'

'Marijke's feeling so much better that she's looking forward to it. We plan to take her to St James's Park to feed the ducks.'

He went away, leaving her to pick up her jacket and handbag and go downstairs. Mr van der Beek was in his study, on the phone; he paused long enough to say, 'I'll be with you in a moment,' and went back to whatever he was talking about. Presently he hung up, picked up his bag and came into the hall. Dobbs was already there, ready to open the door and give her a friendly good morning as they left the house. Mr van der Beek went round the car and opened her door, invited her to get in and settled Basil on the back seat. As he got in beside her, Patience had a chance to look at him. Impeccably turned out as always, but there were tired lines in his face. He started the car without speaking and she sat silent while he drove through the city and out on to the A12. They were nearing Brentwood before she ventured to ask, 'Was the operation a success?'

'Yes. A small setback during the day but everything's all right now.'

'I'm glad. Did you get any sleep? You weren't home when I went to bed.'

She didn't see him smile. 'Oh, yes, I went to bed, and don't worry, I had enough sleep to make me a safe driver.'

'That isn't what I was thinking,' she said indignantly. 'You—you work too hard—I told you you were burning the candle at both ends and you are.' When he didn't say anything she added, 'When I was typing your book I had no idea . . . I imagined you in a splendid consulting-room in Harley Street, sitting with nurses and receptionists running around doing everything for you while you sat behind a desk listening to people complaining about something they hadn't got.'

His chuckle held mockery. 'My dear girl, what a vivid imagination you have. Although I must admit to having rooms in Harley Street I can only confess to one nurse and one receptionist; as to my patients, I'm too busy a man to waste time listening to hypochondriacs. I make sure that is what they are and recommend them to a colleague more fitted to dealing with them than I.'

She refused to be cowed. 'Well, no one would know that just from meeting you. You must be very well known.'

He said without conceit, 'Among members of my profession perhaps; there is no reason why anyone else should consider me well known.'

They had bypassed Chelmsford by now and as they approached Witham he slowed the car. 'Shall we have coffee? There's a nice little pub here—the White Hart.'

The coffee was hot and strong; Patience, making polite conversation, had the leisure to mull over all the things she shouldn't have said. It was too late to do anything about it now and it was obvious that the subject was not to be touched upon again. He kept the talk to trivialities and made no effort to prolong their coffee-drinking. In the car once more, with Basil's head squeezed between them, he asked idly about the aunts, hoped that she would enjoy her stay in Holland and remarked upon the unusually pleasant spring they were having. Patience made suitable replies and brooded over the problem of loving him. It would be nice, she reflected, if one could express one's true feelings and never mind the consequences—like a child. Rosie could put her arms round her uncle's neck and declare that she loved him—something which he obviously enjoyed—but if she were to do it he would recoil in horror. Her face portrayed her thoughts so vividly that Mr van der Beek, glancing sideways at her, asked sharply if she felt all right.

Themelswick looked just as usual as they drove through the village and on to the house. Miss Murch must have been on the look-out for them, for the door was thrown open as he stopped the car before it.

Her welcome was warm. 'There's coffee all ready and waiting and some of my gingerbread. The ladies are in the drawing-room...'

She glanced at Patience and Mr van der Beek said, 'I want a word with Miss Murch, Patience; you go ahead and I'll join you presently.'

The old ladies were delighted to see her, although they wanted to talk about their stay in their old home in preference to hearing about her news. Mrs Perch brought in the coffee, lingered for a moment to ask about her fine job in London, and went away, to be replaced by Mr van der Beek, who said all the right things, drank a cup of coffee and sampled the gingerbread before excusing himself with the plea of business in Norwich.

'I'll be here soon after six o'clock,' he told Patience. 'We'll drive straight back—I'll have to go to the hospital later on this evening.'

He went away, leaving her to explain to the aunts about her trip to Holland.

'How very kind of them to invite you,' murmured Aunt Polly, who, being slightly deaf, had got it all wrong, and Patience, rather than get tangled up in a welter of explanations, let that pass. Her aunts were happy; indeed, they seemed younger, living without worries in their own home again, and it was obvious that Miss Murch was being more than kind. She went to find her presently and thanked her warmly. 'There is not too much work for you?'

Miss Murch bridled. 'Certainly not, Patience. They're real old-fashioned ladies and such as they never give any trouble.' She studied Patience's face. 'You look well. Kept you busy, I dare say—that little Rosie is a handful.'

After lunch Patience went down to the house in the village to fetch her passport and one or two things to supplement her wardrobe. The little house, after the quiet luxury of the house at Chiswick, was depressing; her aunts would be silently unhappy when they had to return to it once more. She shut the door and tried not to think of the future but just be content with the present. Not too difficult; she would be sitting beside Julius in a couple of hours' time and that was enough to blot out everything else.

CHAPTER SEVEN

THE aunts had enjoyed a comfortable snooze while she had been in the village; now they were ready for their tea and a chat.

'You will come back here, dear, when you return from Holland?' Aunt Bessy wanted to know.

It would be cruel to explain that they would all have to go back to the poky little house again; time enough for them to be told when she returned. She replied vaguely and mentioned that she had met Mrs Dodge.

'She misses you both very much,' she told them. 'She would like to be someone's housekeeper now she's widowed—I dare say she is lonely.'

They discussed Mrs Dodge at some length, indeed they were still recalling titbits of kindly village gossip when Mr van der Beek arrived.

He had said soon after six o'clock when he left and he was as good as his word. She went to say goodbye to Miss Murch and receive several messages for Dobbs at the same time, while he sat down with the air of a man who had all the evening before him in which to do nothing, and listened to the old ladies telling him at some length that life for them at the moment was the acme of perfection. Patience, back again, watched him sitting there, to all intents and purposes with nothing more on his mind than the small happenings in Themelswick, while underneath she was quite sure he was aching to be gone.

The aunts paused and she took the opportunity of bidding them goodbye and presently, after various small delays, they got into the car and drove away.

Patience felt Basil's gentle breath on the back of her neck. It reminded her to ask urgently, 'Have you had your tea? I should have thought—and did Basil want a drink?'

He had hardly spoken to her at the house and now he said with a laugh, 'Thank you, I had tea; so did Basil. You enjoyed your day and explained to your aunts?'

'Yes. I had a lovely time. I'm not sure if they quite understood everything, but they're perfectly happy that I should be going to Holland and only too delighted to stay on at the house.'

'Good.' He had no more to say after that, but his silence was friendly and she hesitated to break it. He was driving fast and she guessed that he was anxious to get to the hospital. It didn't matter to her; just sitting beside him made her happy, not completely happy of course, but it would do—it would be better than nothing, and besides she had a good deal to think about herself.

As they reached the outskirts of London she said quietly, 'You want to go to the hospital, don't you? Would you go there first? I can get a bus to Chiswick. It will save you going there and then back again; that would be such a waste of time...'

He said at once, 'I am anxious to go to the hospital as soon as possible but I shan't be there for long—just a quick check-up. We'll go there and you can come in and wait for me. You won't mind a few minutes' delay?'

'Not a bit.'

The hospital was in the heart of the city. He drove into the forecourt, parked in the consultant's bay and invited her to get out.

'What about Basil?'

'He minds the car.' Indeed, the astute animal had already climbed over into the driver's seat. 'Come along.'

The entrance hall was impressive but she was given no time to look around her—she was urged into a lift and, when it stopped, hurried along a corridor and then another with passages left and right so that she was quite confused. If he forgot that she was waiting for him—and he well might—she would never find her way out of the place. She was relieved when he turned into a final passage and thrust aside the swing door at its end, to be met by three people, two youngish men in white coats and a stout middle-aged woman who was undoubtedly Sister. How did they know that Mr van der Beek was coming? she wondered as he introduced her briefly, asked whether she might sit in Sister's office, and left her in the care of a young nurse, who opened the nearby door and invited her inside.

'They won't be long,' she assured Patience as she went. A remark which proved to be over-optimistic; it was three-quarters of an hour before the door opened and Mr van der Beek, now also in a long white coat, marched in with his three companions. It was obvious to her that he had for the moment forgotten that she was there, for he looked surprised before saying carelessly, 'Haven't kept you waiting, have I?'

She felt that she was superfluous. 'I'll wait outside,' she said in her sensible way, and smiled at the youngest of the doctors who was holding the door for her.

There was a kind of foyer outside the office, its window ledge filled with potted plants but not a chair in sight. She wandered to the window and stared out at the darkening evening while she thought of the food she would like to eat. She hoped that Dobbs would have something for them when they eventually got to Chiswick. A drink first, she reflected, then a bowl of soup and perhaps fish or chicken, even a cheese soufflé. She was deciding on a pudding when the office door opened and Mr van der Beek came out, his three companions at his heels.

His, 'Ah, there you are,' was uttered in a voice which conveyed the impression that she had been keeping him waiting, but she forgave him that; she could see that, compared with the welfare of his patient, she fared badly. Anyway, she reminded herself, she had suggested that he should come to the hospital in the first place... besides, she loved him, was head over heels in love with him, and if necessary she would spend the night in the foyer waiting for him. She would have had to, she reminded herself with her usual good sense, for she had no idea how to get out of the place.

Fortunately that was not going to be necessary; another five minutes of murmured conversation and exchanged goodnights and they were in the lift once more and then in the car where Basil yielded up his seat, barking in a satisfied way and then fell asleep on the back seat.

There wasn't a great deal of traffic. Half an hour later they were going through the doorway of his home and there was Dobbs waiting for them with the information that Mijnheer and Mevrouw ter Katte had dined but dinner would be served them at their convenience.

'Oh, ten minutes or so, Dobbs,' said Mr van der Beek. 'I dare say Miss Martin wants to make sure that Rosie is asleep.' He glanced at Patience. 'Come down when you're ready,' he suggested casually. 'Fifteen minutes?'

She watched Basil being led away to his supper, instantly ready, and felt envy, but there was nothing for it but to go upstairs and tidy herself and take a look at Rosie.

The fifteen minutes was barely up when she went downstairs again, and since there was no sign of Mr van der Beek she went into the drawing-room.

'Oh, hello,' Mijnheer ter Katte greeted her cheerfully. 'Julius popped his head round the door but he didn't stay. Have you had a good day? I'll get you a drink. Sherry? Do sit down.'

The sherry was a large one; perhaps she looked as though she needed it. Mevrouw ter Katte begged her to sit down beside her and proceeded to tell her about their own day. Rosie had been an angel—well, for most of the day—and Rinus had been to see Nanny again and it was all arranged that he should fetch her the following afternoon and drive straight on to the ferry. 'Julius hasn't said when he's taking us back home. He told us he'd called in at the hospital this evening and that everything is going well.'

Patience took a very large sip of her sherry; it might play havoc with her empty insides but she was feeling more cheerful already. She tossed off the last of it as Dobbs came to tell her that dinner was served and she got smartly to her feet; being in love hadn't affected her appetite in the least.

The meal was all that she had hoped for; cheese
and cauliflower soup, chicken with a winter salad and
cabinet puddings with a creamy custard, and the conversation was as good as the food. Mr van der Beek,
apparently satisfied with his patient's condition,
carried the talk from one topic to another and none
of it requiring much concentration on her part, which
was a good thing because of the sherry and the excellent Chablis she had drunk with the chicken and
that followed, at his so gentle insistence, by a glass
of Sauternes with the pudding.

The good food and the wine had given her a pretty
colour; her eyes sparkled and since she was happy her
ordinary features took on a prettiness which Mr van
der Beek didn't fail to observe. He wondered idly how
long ago it was when he'd realised that she wasn't a
brown mouse at all.

'Shall we have coffee in the drawing-room?' he
suggested, and they spent the rest of the evening dis-
cussing Rinus's plans for the following day.

'When are we going?' his sister had wanted to know.

'In two days—three at the latest. I'll let you know
for certain tomorrow evening. They're expecting Rinus
in den Haag?'

Presently Patience said goodnight; the three of them
would doubtless have a good deal to discuss and
they would be more comfortable without her. She
thanked Mr van der Beek for her day's outing, assured his sister that she would see to Rosie in the
morning and keep her with her while her father was
making his final arrangements, and went to her room.
It had been a long day but she had enjoyed it. As she
got ready for bed she wondered if she would see much
of Mr van der Beek when they were in Holland. He

was fond of his sister; he would surely come to see her from time to time. On this pleasing thought, Patience fell asleep.

Rosie spent a good deal of the next morning with her parents so that Patience had the chance to sort out the child's clothes and start on packing for them both; she wouldn't know until the evening just when they were going but she would be expected to be ready, and in the afternoon when Rinus ter Katte had gone she began on the far more formidable task of packing his wife's clothes. Mevrouw ter Katte had done a good deal of shopping while she had been in London, extra cases had to be found, and Patience was glad that she had only one case for herself, for the boot would be bulging.

Mr van der Beek arrived home just before dinner. They would leave on the day following the next and, with an eye to Rosie's comfort, they would go from Dover on the short sea route. It would be a longer journey on the other side but, as he pointed out, if she was peevish or feeling sick or needed urgent attention, it could best be done in the car. 'We can stop as often as you like once we are in France,' he pointed out. 'We'll go on the mid-morning ferry.'

He was away all the next day, which gave Patience time to see to the last of the packing, telephone her aunts and wash her hair after she had taken Rosie for a long outing. The little girl was getting excited at the idea of going home again and Patience only hoped that the journey wouldn't be too irksome.

They set off in good spirits although the sight of Basil's woebegone face cast a cloud over everything for Patience, despite Mr van der Beek's assurance that he would be back soon, but she had other things to keep her occupied by the time they reached Dover. Rosie had been dozing quietly beside her but now the bustle of the port wakened her and she started to grizzle. Waiting in the queue to go aboard, Patience did everything she could think of to keep her amused and when finally they were on board Mr van der Beek so thoughtfully saw to it that she and Rosie went to a cabin, where they were brought sandwiches and tea and Rosie ate her way through bread and butter and drank her milk, all smiling complacence. The small meal took up some of the time and the ferry had sailed by the time they had finished it. Brother and sister had gone off together and Patience supposed that she would stay in the cabin with Rosie until they landed. She tucked the moppet into one of the beds and sat down, wishing that she had something to read. Rosie went to sleep almost at once and didn't rouse at the gentle tap on the door.

Mr van der Beek loomed in the doorway. 'Go on deck for half an hour,' he advised her. 'I'll sit with Rosie—Marijke's lying down in the cabin next door. Did you have sufficient to eat? We will stop for tea on our way but get another cup now if you would like. Have you enough money?'

She smiled widely at him, happy because he hadn't forgotten her after all. 'I would like to go on deck if you are sure you don't mind.'

She went away and he watched her go, as neat as a new pin in her sensible jersey dress, not a hair out of place.

She went back to the cabin presently, much refreshed, to find Rosie sitting on her uncle's knee, listening to him story-telling; she had no idea what kind of story it was, for he spoke it in Dutch, but it was

making Rosie crow with laughter. There was just time
to see to her small wants before they rejoined the car
and presently drove ashore, with Rosie still in high
spirits and Mevrouw ter Katte, well rested, talking
non-stop to her brother. Only Patience felt sad; the
journey would soon be over and that probably meant
seeing the last of him. He hadn't told her that she
would no longer be needed once Rosie's nanny was
back, but now that the book was safely with the publisher there was nothing more for her to do. She listened to the child's happy little voice and wondered
about the future; it would be hard to go back to the
little terraced house in Themelswick and take up her
prosaic life again, and it would be even harder for
her aunts.

They crossed into Belgium and then Holland and
Mr van der Beek slowed the car and stopped before
a small wayside café. Tea came in glasses but it was
hot and fragrant and there were crisp little biscuits
too. Patience, occupied with Rosie, took little part in
the conversation. Mr van der Beek looked across the
table at her. 'Not long now,' he told her kindly. 'It
has been a tiring journey for you.'

And his sister chimed in. 'Tomorrow Rosie shall
stay with our housekeeper for a while and I will show
you something of den Haag.'

The ter Kattes had a large solid house surrounded
by a formal garden halfway down a tree-lined avenue
of similar size. Mr van der Beek drew up smoothly
before its front door and got out to help his sister as
an elderly woman came out of the house and down
the short flight of steps to the sweep. The housekeeper, thought Patience, and hoped that they would
like each other. The woman looked almost severe, like

Miss Murch, although she greeted her mistress with pleasure and then came to lift Rosie out of the car. Mr van der Beek, unloading the luggage, paused to introduce her.

'This is Juffrouw Witte, Patience; do you want her to call you Miss Martin or Patience?'

'Patience, please.' They nodded and smiled at each other as she got out of the car and followed the housekeeper into the house. Mevrouw ter Katte was already inside and her husband had come into the hall to greet her but as Patience hesitated in the hall he came to meet her.

'Patience, welcome to our home! Marijke tells me that you have been a great help on the journey and I am so grateful.' There was a young girl in a dark dress hovering at the back of the hall and he called to her. 'This is Bep; she will show you your room, next door to the nursery. When you have tidied yourself and seen to Rosie, come down, and we'll have a drink before dinner.' He went on, 'We dine earlier in Holland, but I dare say you're hungry.'

He kissed his small daughter, said something to Juffrouw Witte and handed Rosie over to Patience. 'Bring her down for a few minutes, will you? Then she can be put to bed and we'll have a quiet evening.'

The nursery and Patience's bedroom were on the second floor at the back of the house, charming rooms, light and airy and very prettily furnished. Patience saw to Rosie and then took her to her own room while she tidied herself, delighted to find that Bep was unpacking her clothes and hanging them away in the fitted wardrobe. She wondered if she would have time to change before dinner; she would have to ask. In the meantime Rosie was to be taken downstairs, presumably to say goodnight before her supper and bed.

Guided by voices, she crossed the hall with Rosie and entered a large high-ceilinged room, its tall windows elaborately draped, a highly polished floor and comfortable chairs and sofas flanked by solid mahogany lamp tables and display cabinets. The ter Kattes were there and so was Mr van der Beek but she didn't say much or stay long; Rosie was hugged and kissed and wished goodnight and then went willingly enough back to Patience.

'Come down as soon as she is asleep,' said Mevrouw ter Katte. 'Don't bother to change tonight.' She smiled at Patience. 'You have been an angel today; to-morrow we'll have a few restful hours.'

Patience bore Rosie back upstairs—a few restful hours sounded nice, and she intended to enjoy them; no one had mentioned days off or free time, but perhaps they might get around to it tomorrow.

She bathed the little girl, tucked her up and waited until she slept, which was only a matter of minutes, before going to her room to do her face and hair; an hour or two in Mr van der Beek's company would be reward enough for her busy day.

He wasn't there. 'Julius has gone home,' explained Mevrouw ter Katte as they sipped their sherry. 'He has to be at an Amsterdam hospital tomorrow morning, quite early; besides he has so many friends here and they will want to see as much as possible of him while he's in Holland. After all, his visit is short.'

So he would go back to England before she did—she would no longer be in his employ, in which case what was to happen to her aunts? Presumably Miss Murch would shake the despised dust of Themelswick off her feet and go back to Chiswick and the house would be closed. The six months were not yet up and he had agreed to rent it for six months, hadn't he? At least they would have the rent before they put it back on the market.

She said politely, 'I expect Mr van der Beek is delighted to see his friends again.'

'He loves his home, too—of course we were brought up there; we go to stay whenever we wish. He has what you call a married couple who look after it when he is not there. I think that sometimes he would like to live there all the time; it would certainly be more suitable a home when he marries. He could go to and fro to England so easily—indeed his work takes him to many countries.'

The only part of this speech Patience had listened to was the bit about him marrying. Did Marijke mean that he planned to marry or was she speaking in general terms—Patience wanted very much to ask, and she was still framing a suitable question when they went in to dinner.

Mevrouw ter Katte was as good as her word in the morning. Patience had dressed and fed Rosie as usual when she came into the nursery.

'I feel so well,' she said happily with the moppet on her lap, 'and now Juffrouw Witte will take Rosie for an hour or two and you and I will go out together. Domus—our gardener—will drive us and I will show you den Haag.'

They didn't go right into the city for, as Mevrouw ter Katte pointed out, Patience could go there by tram if she wanted to see the shops, the Ridderzaal, the Mauritshuis and any of the museums. Instead Domus drove them unhurriedly through the streets until he turned into the Scheveningsweg and towards the sea, going from one end of the boulevard to the other so that Patience might see everything: the Kurhaus with its huge shopping precinct and amusement centre, the hotels and the wide beach with the sea beyond, and at the other end the fishing harbours with fishing-boats moored behind the breakwaters and the ferry terminals. There were one or two fishermen's wives in traditional costume too in their black skirts and shawls and pretty little white caps, mostly older women, for the young ones liked modern dress.

They went to Wassenaar next and stopped for coffee at Auberge de Kieviet, which looked like a country inn but which Patience suspected was both fashionable and expensive, and then they returned to drive back through Scheveningen to Kijkduin where, Mevrouw ter Katte told her, they came in the summer for it was a good deal quieter than Scheveningen. She added regretfully that it was time they returned. 'Rinus will come home to lunch today; his office is in the city and unless he is in the courts he always comes.'

There were parks near the house. Patience took Rosie out after she had given her her midday meal and eaten her own lunch and the rest of the day went quickly. She was to dine downstairs but she took care not to go down to the drawing-room until a few minutes before the meal. She didn't think that nannies dined with the family, although she wasn't sure about that, and there was no one to ask. As it was, she refused a drink, knowing that she would delay dinner if she had one; tomorrow, if there was an opportunity, she would suggest that if it wasn't too much trouble she might have her meal in the nursery; she could always say that Rosie might wake up...

Three days went by, their routine so much like that of Chiswick that Patience sometimes forgot that she was in Holland. The question of dinner had been neatly solved; the ter Kattes had gone out to dine with friends and dinner on a tray for herself seemed logical. Mevrouw ter Katte had wanted her to go down to the dining-room but as Patience pointed out there was no need to give the maid and Juffrouw Witte extra work when she could have her meal in just as much comfort in the nursery, a pleasant cosy room and conveniently close to Rosie. On the next evening old friends had called and stayed to dinner.

She had little time to herself but she was fond of Rosie and enjoyed looking after her; the surroundings were pleasant and when she had some free time she intended to spend it at the shops. She didn't dare to buy much, only necessities, but window-shopping was a pleasant pastime.

She was coming downstairs with Rosie tucked under one arm, dressed for their morning's outing, when Mevrouw ter Katte came out of the drawing-room with Mr van der Beek.

'Here is Julius—he has come to take you both for a drive. Is that not delightful?'

Rosie struggled out of Patience's arms and toddled over to her uncle, crowing with pleasure. Patience, standing on the last stair, hoped that her own overwhelming pleasure wasn't as obvious. She said sedately, 'Good morning, Mr van der Beek.'

He tossed his small niece in the air while she squealed with delight. 'Good morning, Patience. Would it not be a good idea if you were to call me Julius? After all, you are no longer in my employ.'

He spoke casually as though it were a matter of little concern to him.

She flushed. 'Oh, no, of course not—I forgot…very well, Julius.'

'That's better. Shall we go?'

She sat in the back of the car with Rosie, which made it dificult to talk, and in any case Rosie's prattle made conversation unnecessary. She wondered where they were going for once they were clear of the city he turned off the motorway on to a country road, surprisingly rural with flat fields on either side, divided by small canals. There were Friesian cows in abundance and in the distance a windmill and a tall church spire. Very Dutch, reflected Patience. Presently the winding road led into more wooded country, still flat but now there were glimpses of water.

'Lakes,' said Julius over a shoulder. 'They drain into the old Rhine.'

She conjured up the map of Holland she had studied so assiduously before she had left England. 'Between Aalsmeer and Alphen-aan-der-Rijn?' she ventured.

'That's right.'

The road ran alongside the lake now, a tranquil stretch of water bordered by clumps of trees, but presently it dwindled into a canal and Julius turned away from it along a narrow sandy road which led to another lake with a village on its shore. It was nothing more than a large group of small houses, white-walled and red-roofed, but there was a jelly-mould church and a shop in its small centre.

Julius spoke over his shoulder once more. 'Rijnsten,' he said and went through the village, following the road to a clump of trees. There was a wall now, a high brick one pierced by a tall wrought-iron gate standing open. He drove through and along a narrow driveway bordered by thick shrubbery which ended in a wide sweep before a large square house. Its walls were white with a gabled blue slate roof and a great many large windows. The door was open at the top of a double flight of steps, a solid affair with a beautiful fanlight above it. It looked as though it had been there for a very long time and would still be there for many years yet.

'Whose house is this?' asked Patience, staring out through the window.

'Mine. Mine for my lifetime and after that it will be my son's and then his son's. It is the family home.'

He had got out of the car and come round to open her door and lift Rosie out. He tucked his niece under one arm and held out the other hand to Patience. It was a large, firm hand, and the feel of it on hers made her insides tremble. He didn't let it go at once either, but still held it closely looking down at her so searchingly that she asked, 'Is there anything the matter, is something wrong?'

'On the contrary, everything is very right. Come inside, for coffee will be waiting for us and the entire household will be looking forward to spoiling Rosie.'

They mounted the steps and Dobbs appeared as they reached the door. 'This is Dobbs,' said Mr van der Beek, and laughed while Patience stared open-mouthed. 'Dobbs' brother! I'll explain about that later on. Dobbs, this is Miss Martin; Rosie you already know.'

Dobbs smiled widely and stooped and took Rosie from her uncle. 'Indeed we do, sir, and delighted to see her again.'

'Take her along to see Mrs Dobbs, will you? And we would like coffee in the drawing-room.'

Patience was propelled gently across the wide hall and through mahogany double doors into a large room with long narrow windows and a door between them leading to the garden beyond. The door was open and two dogs came in together, great shaggy beasts, their rough coats gleaming, their fearsome sharp teeth showing in what she hoped were grins.

'Josh and Lulabelle,' said Julius, 'Bouviers, mother and son. Offer them a fist.'

They nudged her gently and looked at her with their yellow eyes and she patted their rough heads. 'They look very fierce.'

'They can be, but they will never harm their own and they'll die fighting to protect you. You need never fear them, Patience.'

'They're not at all like Basil...'

He laughed. 'No, but when he comes to live here they'll accept him, just as they've accepted Wisp.' He indicated a small tabby cat asleep on one of the armchairs.

'Why Wisp?'

'Well, she was such a wisp of a thing when they found her.' He urged her towards a small armchair. 'Do sit down; the coffee won't be a minute.'

He sat down near her and the dogs sat one each side of him, and now she had a moment to look about her. The room was beautiful; she supposed one could call it magnificent. It was lived in, though, with books and papers scattered on the small tables and bowls of flowers. The furniture was old and well polished, and the chairs were covered in brocade or velvet in various shades of red, matching the elaborately draped cur-

tains at the windows, and the walls were hung with a
white silky paper. There were a number of paintings
in heavy old-fashioned frames and a vast bow-fronted
display cabinet at the far end of the room.

Mr van der Beek had been watching her narrowly.
'Well?'

'It is quite beautiful. I thought your home in
Chiswick was lovely but this is . . . I know just what
you mean when you say it's your family home.' She
paused. 'You said that Josh and Lulabelle would get
on well with Basil. Are—are you coming to live here
for always?'

He watched her pour their coffee from the tray
Dobbs had brought in. 'Oh, yes, that is to say, instead
of living most of the year in Chiswick and coming
here for a few months, I shall live here and go over
to England once or twice a month. Dobbs and Miss
Murch will remain at Chiswick, of course. I have no
intention of giving up the house there.'

She longed to ask why he intended living at
Rijnsten, although she could guess. He would marry—
he had told her that the house went from father to
son and of course he must wish for a child to take
over from him when the time came. She had never
had any hope that he would fall in love with her, even
like her—but sadness welled up inside her at the
thought of him marrying. It would be to some very
beautiful girl, someone to match his wonderful looks,
who would be the confident hostess of this lovely old
house . . .

'I expect you have a great many patients in
Holland?'

'I have beds in hospitals in den Haag, Amsterdam
and Rotterdam and I visit Utrecht and Groningen

from time to time.' He passed his cup for more coffee.
'Would you like to see something of the house? Rosie
will be quite happy with the Dobbses until lunchtime.
I'll drive you back in time for her supper.'

There was all day ahead of her and in Julius's
company. Never mind the future—that could take care
of itself for the moment—she was going to enjoy every
moment of now.

They wandered through the house together presently: the dining-room, handsome dark furniture and
crimson wallpaper and a beautiful chandelier over the
rectangular table; a small sitting-room—Patience imagined herself sitting there, knitting or sewing—a li-
brary with a small circular staircase at one corner
leading to a narrow gallery above and still more books;
his study with a vast desk littered with papers, and
behind that a billiard room. The staircase curved up
from the hall to a gallery above but he didn't take her
upstairs but led her instead out of a side-door which
opened on to a cobbled yard lined with outbuildings,
on the other side of which there was a wicket gate
which led to the gardens at the back of the house.
She had loved the house and she was enchanted by
the gardens. They had gone through another gate and
were standing in the centre of what would shortly be
a splendid rose garden when hurrying footsteps caused
them to turn round. Coming through the gate was a
girl—no, Patience corrected herself, a woman, and a
very beautiful woman too with dark hair and striking
features, and as she came towards them Patience had
time to note her clothes, simple with the simplicity of
haute couture.

'Julius!' The woman stopped before him, ignoring
Patience, and flung her arms round his neck. Patience

could only guess at what she said next, but it was obvious that she knew Julius well.

Mr van der Beek unwound the arms, his face blandly inscrutable. 'Hello, Sylvia—this is an unexpected pleasure. Patience, this is Mevrouw van Teule—Patience Martin.'

Patience put out a hand and had it shaken in a perfunctory fashion before being ignored. 'Julius, why didn't you tell me you were coming? But now you're here we must dine—this evening?'

'I'm here for a very short time and working for all of it—I'm afraid it won't be possible.'

Mevrouw van Teule stared at Patience. 'Then what is she doing here?' she asked, speaking in English this time.

His eyes were like blue ice but he answered with cool civility. 'Patience has been so kind as to come over with Marijke and keep an eye on Rosie while their nanny has been off ill.'

'Oh, a—what do you say?' She looked at Patience, who answered politely.

'A mother's help, *mevrouw*?'

A small sound escaped Mr van der Beek's lips but all he said in the smoothest of voices was, 'Rosie will be wanting her dinner; we must go back to the house.'

'I'll stay to lunch,' declared Mevrouw van Teule, 'then you'll have someone to talk to.' She smiled enchantingly.

'We shall be delighted, but I must warn you there will be no need for you to make conversation. Rosie is a tremendous talker.'

'The child eats with her nurse, surely?'

'No,' his voice was gentle, 'Rosie has her meals with her family. She will sit between Patience and myself and we shall contrive between us to get her fed.'

'Marijke always had these modern ideas,' she declared. 'Personally I think that children should stay in the nursery until they're old enough to behave themselves.'

Mr van der Beek didn't pursue the subject but led his guests back to the house and into the drawing-room where he offered sherry and made polite small talk until Dobbs came to tell him that lunch was served. 'Rosie is already in her high chair, Mrs Dobbs having seen to her and done the needful.'

'Splendid, Dobbs. Be good enough to set another place for Mevrouw van Teule, will you? She is lunching with us.'

There was a young girl in a plain dress and a white apron standing by Rosie's chair and Mr van der Beek said, 'Ah, Patience, this is Ans, one of Mrs Dobbs' helpers.' He spoke to Ans, who smiled and took the hand Patience offered, nodded her head cheerfully and went away.

Patience, bidden to sit down beside Rosie, did so, and was instantly subjected to a steady flow of chatter, to all of which she nodded understandingly without understanding one word, while Julius and his guest, he at the head of his table, she beside him opposite Patience, kept up a steady if desultory conversation.

Lunch, thought Patience, spooning soup into the small mouth, wasn't going to be quite what she had expected and hoped for.

CHAPTER EIGHT

MR VAN DER BEEK was an accomplished host. He contrived to listen with apparent interest to whatever Mevrouw van Teule had to say while at the same time joining in the rather one-sided conversation Rosie and Patience were enjoying. Mevrouw van Teule had said, '*Dag,*' to Rosie and then ignored her; she had ignored the dogs, too, neither of whom made any movement towards her; indeed they sat side by side on the side furthest away from her during the meal, not making a sound but rolling their yellow eyes at Patience from time to time, their tongues hanging out in what she thought hopefully were friendly grins.

She had little to say during the meal; she had no intention of competing with the other woman and when Julius addressed her she replied readily but forbore from making any remarks of her own, only low-voiced wheedlings to Rosie, who tended to frown fiercely across the table at her uncle's guest, at the same time keeping up a continuous chatter between mouthfuls.

'Doesn't that child ever stop talking?' Mevrouw van Teule asked Patience sharply, aware that she had by no means secured the whole of Julius's attention.

'Well, you see,' explained Patience carefully, 'she's still very small and she's just discovered what fun it is to talk. She's such a happy child and such fun...'

Mevrouw van Teule shrugged elegant shoulders. 'I suppose if you earn your living looking after children you get to like them,' she laughed. 'You would need to, wouldn't you?'

'Indeed yes,' said Patience in a chilly voice. 'Just as if the children were your own you would get to like them too—if you saw enough of them.' Her smile was charming and Mr van der Beek, sitting back in his chair, allowed himself a faint smile. He leaned from his chair, lifted Rosie on to his knee and offered her a bon-bon from the little silver dish on the table. Mevrouw van Teule made an impatient sound and Patience gave him a limpid look from her beautiful eyes. She hoped that he knew what he was marrying—he must love the woman very much; perhaps if she loved him too she would change. Highly unlikely, reflected Patience, having second thoughts.

After lunch Patience said, in her matter-of-fact way, 'Rosie usually rests for an hour; is there a room where she can lie down? I'll stay with her.'

She hated to go away and leave the two of them together but her instinct told her that was what they wanted, certainly Mevrouw van Teule did. But not, it seemed, Julius. 'She can go to bed a little earlier,' he said easily. 'We'll take her down to the gardener's house. I've a surprise for her there—a donkey, for her to ride.' He glanced at her feet. 'Good, you're wearing sensible shoes—it's rather muddy. There's an old jacket you can borrow.'

He turned to Mevrouw van Teule. 'You'll forgive us, Sylvia? It is the only time I shall have and I have to go back to Amsterdam this evening—work.'

She smiled with a charming wistfulness. 'Oh, Julius, I had hoped that we might have time together. When are you going back to England?'

'It depends very much on my patients.' He glanced at Patience. 'Will you ring that bell by the fireplace, please? Dobbs will get Ans to show you where you can see to Rosie—I'll be here waiting for you.'

Patience said, 'Very well,' and bade the other woman goodbye before going off with Ans, who showed them into a well equipped cloakroom hidden away by the staircase. She wished she knew how to reprimand Rosie for refusing to look at Mevrouw van Teule and even, horror of horrors, putting out a small pink tongue as she was borne away. Unnoticed, Patience hoped.

The pair of them went back to the hall presently and found Julius sitting on a table, deep in thought. He got up when they reached him.

'Of course, little girls who put their tongues out at guests don't deserve treats.' He spoke in English and Rosie blew him a kiss and giggled.

'Oh, I did hope no one saw it. I would have told her how rude it was only I don't know enough Dutch.'

'Leave it to me.' He lifted Rosie on to the table and put his arms around her and whatever he said couldn't have been very severe because she gave him a kiss.

There was no sign of Mevrouw van Teule; Patience wondered what they had said to each other before she left. Mr van der Beek smiled and was looking smug; perhaps they had made a date after all . . .

He took them through the side-door again, past the outbuildings and down a path to the side of the gardens, hedged with shrubs. At its end he opened a door in a high brick wall which opened into the kitchen garden, a place of incredible neatness with rows of vegetables sprouting and not a weed in sight. There were trees there too, apple and pear and plum and a whole square of fruit bushes. Patience would have liked to linger but Julius was striding ahead with Rosie on one arm towards another door. This one opened on to a paddock at the other end of which was a small house, smoke curling from its chimney, washing blowing from a long clothes line, and from the far end came two horses and a small donkey, ambling towards them.

They stood still to watch them. 'Do you ride?' asked Mr van der Beek.

'Not since my mother and father died—I had a pony. What are their names?'

'Jess and Caesar. Jess is the gentlest little lady, not up to my weight though—Marijke rides her when she's staying here.'

'And Caesar is yours?'

'Yes. I thought Rosie may like to name the donkey; she's only been with us for a few days.'

'Had she no name?'

'I came across her being driven to the knacker's yard.'

'Oh, the poor little beast—how kind of you, Julius.' She gave him a glowing look. 'Now she will be happy for the rest of her life.'

He didn't answer but took some lumps of sugar from his pocket and, rather surprisingly, a carrot. The horses had their sugar and Rosie, armed with the carrot and safely in her uncle's arms, offered the donkey the carrot.

'Oh, she is so pretty,' said Patience, and Rosie echoed,

'Pretty, pretty, pretty.'

'So "Pretty" it is to be, and here comes Jon with the saddle.'

The donkey was new to a saddle, new for that matter to a small person on her back, but she raised no objections and stood obediently while Rosie was sat gently down and then led slowly around the field, her uncle on one side, Patience on the other, Jon and the horses following behind. Presently Mr van der Beek said, 'Well, that will do for today. Jon, saddle her up for a short time each day, will you; put your youngest on her back for a short while so that when Rosie comes again she will find it easy.'

He paused to say it all over again for Patience's benefit, talked for a few minutes with the man then watched while Pretty and her two companions wandered off again. Rosie watched her go too and then burst into tears, having been under the impression that Pretty would return with her to her home.

Patience picked her up. 'Darling, Pretty has to have her tea and go to bed just as you do. You shall come again very soon and Uncle Julius will let you ride her.' All this in English, which, strangely enough, Rosie had no difficulty in understanding.

'The pity of it is,' Uncle Julius observed, 'that I am going back to England tomorrow.'

Patience spun round, clutching Rosie. 'Tomorrow? But I thought you'd be here for—it's only a week...'

He stood looking down at her. 'Well, well—and will you mind if I am not here, Patience?'

'No. No, of course not, why should I?' She refused to look at him. 'You were going to tell me about Dobbs and his brother.'

He accepted the change of subject with apparent unconcern. 'So I was. A simple story really. I had an English grandmother who left me the house in Chiswick. Dobbs had been her chauffeur for years and I took him on with the house. Miss Murch joined us in answer to my advertisement and they deal excellently with each other. Mr father's manservant died shortly after him and since Dobbs had a brother looking for work in England I took him on here. He fell in love with my cook—an admirable state of affairs, you must admit.'

'What will Dobbs do if you come to live here?'

'I hope he will marry Miss Murch; their romance has been blossoming for some years now. They can stay on as caretakers. I never know when I may have to go to England and I have friends there.'

She knew nothing about him, she reflected as they walked slowly back to the house. She knew where he lived and what he did but she was no nearer to knowing him as a person: what he thought, what he wanted from his life, whether he was loved—and then there was his habit of never mentioning his plans until the last minute . . . not that it was any of her business, she reminded herself honestly. It seemed likely that she wouldn't see him again. He wouldn't be going back to Themelswick now that the book was finished and there would be no Rosie for her to mind in Chiswick. She would return to England when she was no longer needed by the ter Kattes and make her way back to the aunts.

'You're very deep in thought,' remarked Julius as they reached the house. 'You need a cup of tea to revive you. We'll have it in the drawing-room. You take Rosie and tidy her up and I'll dry off the dogs.'

They had gone in through the side-door again and he turned away to one of the rooms behind the kitchen, the dogs at his heels, while she went through to the hall and into the cloakroom, where she washed Rosie's tear-stained face, combed her fair hair and then did her own face, pushing her hair back ruthlessly from her face. It did not matter, she told herself bitterly, what she looked like. Her lack of looks seemed worse than ever since she had met Mevrouw van Teule, and the sooner she stopped mooning over Julius van der Beek, the better. A resolution that she carried out with such strictness that he decided that it would be the wrong moment to suggest, with a suitable vagueness, some tentative ideas as to her future.

He betrayed none of these thoughts during tea, a meal designed to please little Rosie although there were sandwiches for the grown-ups and a large fruit cake also. One of Miss Murch's recipes, confided Dobbs, sent to his wife so that Mr van der Beek would be able to enjoy it. He was partial to cake, added Dobbs *sotto voce*.

Presently Rosie was borne away by her uncle to say goodbye to Mrs Dobbs in her kitchen, leaving Patience free to look around her. It struck her then more forcibly than ever that Mr van der Beek was a man of wealth. Another good reason why she should forget him as quickly as possible.

Rosie sat on Patience's lap as they drove back to den Haag, half asleep, rousing from time to time to chatter about her day, but Mr van der Beek had nothing to say and nor did Patience save for soft murmuring replies to Rosie. Once at the house, he didn't linger. Patience had taken Rosie straight upstairs after greeting her mother and father, to take off her jacket before carrying her down again to say goodnight before her supper. Julius was on the point of going, standing talking to his sister and Rinus in the hall, but he glanced up as she reached the bottom of the staircase and crossed over the hall to stand before her.

'A lovely day,' he said softly and bent to kiss his niece, and then very deliberately kissed Patience. No one had kissed her like that before; indeed she had seldom been kissed—quick pecks on a cheek which had meant nothing either to her or the pecker—but Julius's kiss was something different; rather like an electric shock, she thought bemusedly. Of course he must have had a lot of practice with beautiful creatures like Sylvia van Teule, who would have known how to accept it gracefully. It was regrettable that she just stood there, gazing up into his face, with her mouth slightly open. It would have helped if he had tossed some light-hearted remark at her, she thought crossly; as it was he looked at her for a long moment and went back to his sister and then, within moments, had gone out of the house. He hadn't even said goodbye.

She presented Rosie for goodnight hugs and kisses and went back upstairs to put her to bed the moment she had had her supper. 'Sing,' demanded Rosie, warm and fragrant from her bath, tucked into her bed. So Patience sang, her voice rather wobbly because she wanted very much to have a good cry.

'Such a pity,' observed Marijke at dinner, 'that Julius has to return—he planned to stay for several more days. I wonder why he decided to return to Chiswick. Did you have a pleasant day, Patience? There was almost no time to talk of it. There is a new donkey, is there not? Did Rosie like that?'

'Oh, very much, she wasn't in the least bit afraid; indeed she cried a good deal when we went back to the house.'

'She was good with her dinner? She ate everything and behaved nicely?'

'Yes. She was a very good girl.'

'Just the three of you?'

'Well, no. A Mevrouw van Teule called and she stayed to lunch.'

'Sylvia van Teule. She has—how do you say?—the claws in Julius—a widow and really most anxious to marry again. Rosie does not like her; she was not rude?'

'No, no.'

'Bah!' said Marijke with some force. 'She does not like little children but she is very beautiful and chic.'

Patience agreed in her pleasant voice, wishing uncharitably that Mevrouw van Teule would come out in spots or develop a squint. Not that it mattered any more. Julius had gone and his future held no interest for her.

Julius wasn't mentioned at all during the next few days; Patience put him out of her mind—only he kept popping back in—and concentrated on being a good nanny. She had grown very fond of Rosie and she liked the ter Kattes and although she didn't have much time to herself she found herself with a whole day off on her own while they took Rosie to Utrecht to see Rinus's parents. She had money in her purse and it was a fine day; she bade Juffrouw Witte goodbye for the moment and took a tram to the shops. This might be her only chance of buying presents for the aunts and something suitable for Mrs Dodge and perhaps Miss Murch. She had been told about the Bijenkorf and she spent a delightful hour there, roaming round the various counters, choosing scarves for the aunts, a Delft blue model windmill for Mrs Dodge, who liked ornaments on the mantelpiece, and, upon reflection, a bottle of Boldoot eau-de-cologne for Miss Murch. She stopped for coffee too, taking her time over it since she had all day, and presently she wandered down one of the arcades to study the expensive clothes in the smart boutiques. She was admiring an evening gown in one window when the shop door opened and Mevrouw van Teule came out. She stopped when she saw Patience and then smiled.

'The little mother's help,' she said gaily. 'You have a day off?' Her eye took in the parcels from the Bijenkorf as the smile became scornful. 'You have done your shopping? Little gifts to take home perhaps? It is a good shop for such things, especially if one has not got too much money.'

She paused. 'You have half an hour to spare? Will you come and have coffee with me? I am tired after a dress fitting and need to rest for a while. There is a coffee-shop close by...'

It was difficult to refuse without being rude. Patience went with her to the end of the arcade at

which there was an elegant tea shop where they sat
down at a table in a room all pink lampshades and
elaborate curtains and an ankle-deep carpet and
haughty waitresses.

Mevrouw van Teule ordered coffee. 'You will have
a cake? I do not dare.' Her smile was faintly ma-
licious. 'But for you it will not matter; you have no
shape.' She glanced down at her own generous curves
and Patience, whose shape was a quite charming one,
said cheerfully,

'Well, I don't need to diet, but I won't have a cake,
thank you.'

She drank her coffee with whipped cream and plenty
of sugar and felt sorry for her companion, sipping
black coffee without much pleasure.

'How did you come to know Mr van der Beek?'
asked Mevrouw van Teule. 'Perhaps through his sister
who employs you?'

'No, I worked for him in England.'

Mevrouw van Teule opened her eyes wide. 'Really?
He didn't tell me—in his household, perhaps?'

'Yes.'

Her companion nodded. 'Of course! It was through
him you became employed by Marijke ter Katte.' She
smiled sweetly. 'I shall hear all about you when he
returns. He does not like to be away from me for too
long. It will be easier for both of us when he returns
to live here in Holland. I dislike the journey to
England and I do not much care for London, although
some of the dress shops are excellent and your Harrods
is a splendid place. I dare say you don't shop there?'

'No, I don't.' Patience spoke quietly, wondering
how she could get away from the woman. She allowed

her eyes to stray to the clock on the café wall and
said, 'My goodness, is that the time? I promised
Juffrouw Witte that I would be back for lunch. I catch
a tram from the end of Lange Vooruit.' She managed
a smile. 'Thank you for the coffee, it was delicious.'

'Run along,' said Mevrouw van Teule in a patron-
ising voice which set Patience's teeth on edge. 'It was
so nice meeting you. I must tell Julius—Mr van der
Beek.'

Patience went, conscious of the woman's eyes on
her, pricing her clothes, having scathing thoughts
about her make-up and hair. Well, I don't care, she
thought, hurrying in the direction of the tram although
she had no intention of catching it, Only I wish she
hadn't said all that about Julius. They must know
each other very well and he's coming back to see her.
Did he really not like to be away from her? she wondered. It had been impossible to guess at his feelings
that afternoon at Rijnsten; she had always found it
difficult to know what he was thinking behind that
bland face. They had, after all, been alone for ten
minutes or more while she was with Rosie—time
enough to make plans...

Sufficiently far away from the arcades, she spent a
blissful hour in the Mauritshuis, gazing her fill of
Rembrandts, Vermeers and a host of famous Dutch
painters. She was too absorbed to remember to have
lunch but the tea Juffrouw Witte had ready for her
more than made up for that.

Being in love, she should have been pining and off
her food, she reflected, making short work of sandwiches, buttered toast and delicious little scones and

cakes. Perhaps she wasn't in love, only infatuated. Only she knew that wasn't true.

It was a good thing that the ter Kattes and Rosie came home then, for she was fast falling into the dumps.

Several days later Mevrouw ter Katte came out of the drawing-room as Patience was taking Rosie upstairs after their morning outing. 'Patience, will you let Juffrouw Witte have Rosie for a little while? I wish to talk to you. It is still too early for her dinner and she can go to the kitchen off Juffrouw Witte's room.'

Patience came downstairs again. 'Very well, *mevrouw*, but Rosie needs one or two things done first. Shall I see to that and bring her down again—about five minutes?'

'Yes, yes, of course. Come into the drawing-room when you're ready.'

Nanny is coming back, reflected Patience, unbuttoning Rosie's outdoor garments, changing her small shoes and combing her hair. She smoothed her own tidy head, bore Rosie down to the kitchen and went back to the drawing-room.

Mevrouw ter Katte patted the sofa beside her. 'Ah, Patience. Rinus has been to the hospital and seen Nanny and has also talked to the doctors—she went there to have a complete check-up before she starts work again and she has been pronounced quite fit. She will come back here—let me see—it is Tuesday today, she will be back on Friday. Would you like to go back to England on Saturday? Rinus will arrange your tickets.'

'I'm glad Nanny is quite better; Rosie will be glad to see her again. Would it not be a good idea if I were to go back on Friday before Nanny comes? I'd love to meet her but I do wonder if it would be easier for Rosie to understand if we just exchange places, as it were; if she wonders where I am she will have Nanny to comfort her and explain—anyway she hasn't known me long and she will forget me quickly. May I tell her that Nanny is coming back?'

'Will she understand?'

'Oh, yes, we understand each other very well in a basic kind of way.' She smiled at Mevrouw ter Katte, who was looking uneasy. 'I've very much enjoyed looking after Rosie, but I knew it was temporary when I said I'd help out.'

'You do not feel,' Mevrouw ter Katte sought for a word, 'cast out?'

'Certainly not. I must go home to my aunts and get them settled again.'

She saw the relief on her companion's face. 'We have enjoyed your stay here, Patience, and we are very grateful, and I think that it is a good idea that you should return to England before Nanny comes back, for Rosie's sake. She is fond of you.'

'Yes, but she's fond of Nanny, as I said; she will be very happy to see her again.'

'And you, you will find more work?'

'Well, not at once—I've been living with my great-aunts for some time now and I see to the house and so on; for a time at least I won't have the opportunity to look for a job.'

'Your aunts are at the house Julius rented, are they not?'

'When I go back they will leave there. Miss Murch will go back to Chiswick and I expect that the house will go on the market again as soon as the six months are up.'

'That is most satisfactory,' said Mevrouw ter Katte, glad to have the matter settled, 'and now I will not keep you any longer. I'm sure Rosie wishes for her dinner. It will be very nice when the baby is here and I feel well enough to do more. I am not usually like this.'

'Well, it is only a few more weeks, isn't it? I expect you hope for a son.'

'Indeed we do. If you ever return to Holland, Patience, you must come and see us.'

'I should like that,' said Patience cheerfully, knowing that her chances of coming were slim. 'I'll go and get Rosie, shall I?'

Mevrouw ter Katte nodded, 'Rinus will let you know about your tickets and the times of the ferry and the train. Would you ask Juffrouw Witte to come here, please? We must arrange for Nanny's return.'

With Rosie tucked up in bed and asleep that night, Patience went to her room and sat down to think. She would have to pack within the next day or so; that would be easy enough for she had bought very little while she had been in den Haag. She would have to write to the aunts and post the letter in the morning. Telephoning them was of little use, for they disliked the instrument and they were deaf. She hoped that Miss Murch wouldn't mind them staying one more night while she opened up the terraced house and did some shopping; she would have to make a list. And money—she got her handbag and counted its contents. She wasn't sure if she was expected to pay her fare back and she hadn't liked to ask, but, even if

that were the case, she still had a respectable sum
saved. She found pen and paper and began on the
task of arranging her finances so that they could live
without worry until the house was sold or let once
more.

Friday came. She was to leave in the morning.
Mijnheer ter Katte had decided that it would be easier
for her if she went back by plane and had booked her
a seat on a late morning flight. That way, he explained kindly, she would be able to reach her home
sometime during the afternoon. He himself would
drive her to Schiphol and see her safely on board. He
had given her an envelope with her ticket and when
she opened it there was money inside, enough to pay
for her train fare to Norfolk and the journey into
London from Heathrow. 'I do not like you to be alone
in London,' said Rinus gravely, 'so you will please
take a taxi and when you arrive home will you telephone us?'

She was touched by his thoughtfulness. 'Yes, of
course I will, and I'll take a taxi too. I shall be home
about teatime.' She went away to pack the last of her
belongings and peer inside the small package Mevrouw
ter Katte had given her. A locket on a gold chain and
inside the locket a coloured photo of Rosie. Patience
felt like crying but there wasn't time; she went back
downstairs where everyone was assembled to wish her
goodbye and contrived very nicely to smile and shake
hands and hug Rosie who, cheerfully unaware of what
was happening, kissed her with a good deal of
giggling.

'Oh, you must come again, Patience,' said Mevrouw
ter Katte, kissing her too.

'That would be nice,' said Patience inadequately. 'Perhaps I shall one day.'

They didn't have to wait too long at Schiphol; she bade goodbye to Mijnheer ter Katte and went away towards Customs, not looking back, because she knew that looking back got you nowhere. She drank the coffee she was offered on board, read the leaflets from cover to cover and took care not to look out of the window at a fast-receding Holland. She wouldn't see it again, and since Julius was going to live there she wouldn't see him again either.

Her case was one of the first on the carousel and Customs merely nodded her through. She emerged into the vast crowded reception area and the first person she saw was Mr van der Beek.

Unlike her, he showed no surprise, but took her case in one hand and her arm in the other and marched her out to the Bentley.

'Just a minute,' said Patience, subduing delight at the sight of him, 'I am on my way home—there is no need...'

'Get in,' said Mr van der Beek, in a no-nonsense voice. 'I intended to go over to fetch you but I had an emergency operation—Rinus told me which plane you would be on. I'll drive you up to Themelswick.'

She had got in; she had no choice—a gentle push from behind had seen to that—but she still protested. 'I am expected home about teatime—there is no need...'

He got in beside her. 'You said that just now; besides, I want to go there myself and make a few arrangements with Miss Murch. Fasten your seatbelt, Patience.'

She did as she was told, feeling that the situation was a little out of hand, but it was important not to argue at the moment; he was already out of the airport, making for the M25. She sat quietly, fuming and at the same time bemused with the happiness of seeing him again.

As he turned off the motorway at St Albans in the direction of Ware and the A10 he spoke for the first time, breaking a lengthy silence. 'We'll talk over lunch.'

It was more than half an hour later when he had turned off the A10 in an easterly direction and joined the A11. North of Newmarket he took a side-road and stopped the car in Mildenhall. The Bell was an old coaching inn, cosy and quiet. They ate roast beef, Yorkshire pudding and simply delicious crisp roast potatoes and followed these with treacle pudding as light as air. They drank a bottle of Perrier water between them and finished with a pot of coffee. Patience, who had been seething with curiosity and annoyance at his arbitrary behaviour, sensibly subdued these feelings and enjoyed her meal. It was only as they went back to the car that she remembered he had said that he would explain while they ate, but she was aware that he hadn't; he had talked about everything under the sun but ignored the situation. In the car she said sharply, 'You were going to explain ...'

'Have I not done so?' he wanted to know mildly. 'Besides the things I want to talk about are best not discussed while I'm driving; for one thing I want to see your face ...'

She turned her head and studied his profile; he was staring ahead and he looked stern. There was no point in annoying him—at any rate at the speed they were driving they would be in Themelswick in rather more than an hour. She sat quietly, watching the countryside, and unbidden thoughts of Mevrouw van Teule roared round her head. Her delight at being with Julius faded; of course he hadn't come to Heathrow specially to drive her back—had he not said that he had had to go there himself? She supposed that Rinus had told him which flight she would be on and he had decided that he might as well give her a lift. He was a kind man despite his aloofness.

She smiled involuntarily as he stopped the car before the house. It looked the same although she was quick to see that someone had done a good deal of work on the flowerbeds and the lawn was close cut.

Mr van der Beek got out and opened her door. 'Go in and see your aunts,' he said. 'I'll join you presently.'

He turned away to get her case from the boot and she went in through the half-open door to meet Miss Murch advancing down the hall.

'Good afternoon, Patience,' said the housekeeper graciously. 'How well you look. Your aunts are in the drawing-room. I'll bring tea in a few minutes. Is Mr van der Beek outside still?'

'Yes, Miss Murch. I hope you are well?'

'Thank you, yes, and delighted at the prospect of returning to Chiswick at last.'

Well, at least one person is delighted and going to be happy, thought Patience, and opened the drawing-room door.

The aunts were pleased to see her. 'My dear Patience,' observed Aunt Bessy, 'how very well you are looking—plumper too. I have always considered that you would be improved with a nicely rounded bosom...' She looked over Patience's shoulder. 'Ah, Mr van der Beek, how delightful to see you again.'

Patience bent over Aunt Polly. Had he heard Aunt Bessy's rather penetrating voice making remarks about her bosom? She did hope not.

Nothing in his manner betrayed the fact that he had. 'You are staying for a few days?' enquired Aunt Bessy. 'We shall be delighted if you do.' She turned to Patience. 'Pour the tea, will you, my dear? I'm sure Mr van der Beek would enjoy a cup.'

He sat down between the two old ladies and listened to Patience answering their questions. Had she been to many parties? Was there a good theatre in den Haag? Whom had she met?

She answered them as carefully, never once mentioning the fact that she had been a temporary nanny, something they had quite forgotten. Presently Aunt Polly asked again, 'You will stay, Mr van der Beek.'

'I'm afraid not. I have to return at once—I'm going over to Holland tonight.'

Patience put her cup down very quietly. 'For always?' she asked.

'No, just a quick visit—a personal matter.'

Recklessness took hold of her tongue. 'Of course—I met Mevrouw van Teule in den Haag, we had coffee together, and she told me that you would be going back as soon as you could. It must be very difficult for you both being apart. How fortunate that the journey is so short. It's a great pity that she dislikes London though, but of course if you are going to live in Holland that won't matter, will it?'

He was looking at her thoughtfully, his eyes gleaming with amusement. 'No, it won't matter in the slightest.' He got up. 'I must be off.' He bade the old ladies goodbye and turned to Patience. 'Come to the door with me, Patience?' When they were alone he said, 'I have no time to untangle the muddle you are in, but I'll be back.'

'There's no need.' She spoke fiercely; having burned her boats she couldn't care less what happened now. 'There is no need for us ever to see each other again.'

He stood over her, staring down into her face, and she returned his look steadily although her hands were tightly clasped. He laughed, then went out to his car and got in and drove away, and she shut the door slowly. Shutting him out of her life.

CHAPTER NINE

PATIENCE went back to the drawing-room and poured more tea for her aunts.

'A charming man,' declared Aunt Bessy. 'Such a pity he could not stay! Doubtless he leads a very busy life. Did I hear you say that he was going back to Holland this evening? An urgent matter, no doubt.'

'Very urgent,' said Patience, with such a snap that both ladies looked at her.

'You must be tired, dear,' said Aunt Polly kindly. 'Such a long journey. How strange to think that you were in Holland only this morning.'

Presently Patience went in search of Miss Murch to thank her for her tea and tell her that she was going down to the village. 'I must get the house ready for my aunts; it's been closed for several weeks and I'll need to air it as well as making up the beds.'

Miss Murch, at the kitchen table picking over some gooseberries, wouldn't hear of it. 'There's a room for you here all ready—go down there in the morning if you must, but tonight you'll sleep in comfort here and have a good wholesome supper before you go to bed. Besides, what will your aunts think, the poor ladies, if you go off again just as soon as you've got here?'

So Patience unpacked what she needed for the night and went back to the drawing-room to listen to her aunts' recounting of the events which had taken place

in the village since she had gone away. It took up the
whole of the evening until they had had their supper
and she had seen them safely into their beds; only
then did she have the leisure to think her own
thoughts, and they were so sad that she went to bed
herself after helping Miss Murch with the washing-
up. She was tired. It had indeed been a long day, cul-
minating in her outburst about Mevrouw van Teule.
She should have bitten her tongue before she had uttered one word about the woman and now not only
was she not going to see Julius again, they had parted
on bad terms. Tired though she was, it took her a
long time to get to sleep. She woke in the night and
allowed herself the luxury of a good cry before
dropping off again.

She had breakfasted, settled her aunts in the
drawing-room, helped with the dishes and was about
to leave the house when Mr Bennett, driving a car as
old as himself, arrived.

'Ah, my dear Patience. You are just going out? I
must ask you to wait for a while for I have something
to say to you. Good news, I am glad to say.'

She led the way indoors. 'Would you like to talk
to the aunts?' she asked. 'I was just on my way to the
house to get it ready for them . . .'

He stood in the hall while she took his hat and coat.
'No need, my dear. Not for the moment at least. The
house has been bought subject to its becoming vacant
when Mr van der Beek's lease expires, and he has expressed the wish that until then your aunts should
remain here.'

'That's several weeks . . .'

'Indeed it is.'

She sat him down in a chair. 'Who is the new owner? And does he agree?'

'Yes, yes. He will, in fact, be contacting you very shortly; in the meantime Mr van der Beek does not wish the house to be empty. His request that you should remain until the house changes hands seems to me to be a reasonable one.'

'What about Miss Murch—his housekeeper?'

'She is to return to his London home. He has asked me if Mrs Dodge would consider taking up residence here for the time being.'

'What about the house in the village? It'll be empty.'

'For the moment, yes. I should mention that this house has been sold for a comfortable figure; the capital, wisely invested, will mean that your aunts can live in more comfort.' He added gently, 'That is, I think, an important aspect of the matter.'

She felt guilty. 'Yes, of course it is. I'm glad for them and I don't want them worried. Thank you very much for coming, Mr Bennett. Do you suppose that I should give our landlord notice? I mean, the aunts have always disliked living there; perhaps we could afford to find something more to their liking. Would there be time before we have to leave here?'

'That is difficult to say. I suggest that you leave things as they are for the moment.'

'Very well. All the same, I think I'll go down to the village each day and air the place and clean up a little, just in case we have to go there before we can find something better.'

Mr Bennett, after due thought, agreed to this, and she urged him to go to the drawing-room and see the aunts while she fetched coffee for them all. In the kitchen she asked, 'Did you know that this house had been sold, Miss Murch? My aunts are to stay here until the new owner moves in. Mr van der Beek has asked if they would do that.'

Miss Murch put the coffee on the tray. 'Yes, I knew. That Mrs Dodge is coming up here to take care of things—you'll be able to manage between you, I've no doubt.'

'You're not going yet?'

'Tomorrow.' Her severe features broke into a smile.

'Mr Dobbs will be glad,' said Patience, and Miss Murch looked arch.

'That's as may be, Patience. I must say I can't wait to get back to a civilised community and a decent butcher.'

Patience let that pass and bore the coffee tray to the drawing-room, where she found Mr Bennett endeavouring to make the aunts understand something of their changed circumstances. They listened to him politely but interrupted from time to time to talk about something quite different so that presently Patience said, 'Never mind, Mr Bennett, I'll explain a bit at a time. By the time we leave here they'll be used to the idea.'

She saw him to the door presently. 'You have no idea when the new owner will call?' she asked him. 'Won't there be papers to sign?'

'Yes, I am preparing them, but these things take a little time. When the contracts are drawn up I will bring them for your Aunt Bessy to sign. The house is in her name, is it not?'

Patience nodded. 'Oh, well I dare say he'll let us know when it is he is coming.'

Mr Bennett got into his car and started the engine in a cautious manner; he would have been happier in a pony and trap, thought Patience, watching him drive slowly away. She waved before he turned off into the road; he had looked after her aunts' affairs for a very long time and she was fond of him.

She spent the rest of the day helping Miss Murch to pack, listening the while to a great deal of advice as to how best to run the house. 'I know that Mrs Dodge is coming,' said Miss Murch with a ladylike sniff, 'but it's a house that needs careful housekeeping.'

Patience, folding sensible nightgowns, murmured a nothing. Mrs Dodge, while not a cordon bleu cook and unused to a London establishment, would make an excellent housekeeper. It would be nice if the new owner kept her on. She had been widowed for some years now and life hadn't been easy; her shabby little house was in an even worse state than the one Patience and her aunts lived in. She would mention it, if and when the man came. She had forgotten to ask if he was a family man. More than likely; the house was large for one person to live in. True, Mr van der Beek had lived alone save for Miss Murch and her helpers and herself, but then he had been writing a learned book which required special solitude... She started to move Miss Murch's sombre dresses from the wardrobe, reminding herself that she really must stop thinking about him. Had she not shut the door on him? So why couldn't she shut her mind on him too?

The next morning she went down to the village. The little house looked shabbier than ever and when she went in it felt damp and cold and airless. She walked through the poky rooms, deciding what needed to be done before going back to say goodbye to Miss Murch.

'Please remember me to Dobbs,' said Patience as they shook hands. 'He was very kind to me when I was at Chiswick.' She saw the housekeeper off, standing outside the house and waving until the taxi was out of sight.

Mrs Dodge wasn't coming until the following day. Patience got the tea, saw her aunts comfortably settled with their books and knitting and repaired to the kitchen to cook the supper. It was nice being back in her old home but she felt uneasy; the sooner she knew just how long they were to stay there, the better she would be pleased.

Mrs Dodge arrived the next morning. She knew very little more than Patience but she was delighted to have a job, even if only for a short time. The money, she confided to Patience, was good, enough for her to put some by. They spent some time working out the household budget and, armed with a long list of groceries and the promise to bring them back with her when she returned from the village later that day, Patience, in a dress which had seen better days but was very neat all the same, went off to the little house in the village.

She was glad to have something to do; it kept her mind off her sad thoughts. She opened windows, washed curtains and hoovered and polished, determined to make the little house as much like home as possible.

She had brought sandwiches with her and there was tea in the tea caddy; she had a whisk round and a quick lunch, did her shopping and tackled the contents of the linen cupboard before going back to spend the evening with her aunts and presently tumble thankfully into bed.

It was a splendid opportunity to turn the little house inside out and upside down; her aunts were quite content to remain with Mrs Dodge to see to their needs, and the weather was fine, too, so that anything she could haul out into the tiny back garden could get a good airing. By the end of a week there wasn't much left to do. There was still no news from the new owner; she couldn't stock the larder or make up the beds but there was one job she could tackle. Above the tiny landing there was access to the loft where her aunts' heavy old trunks had been housed when they had moved. They contained various personal treasures of the old ladies which had been deemed unsuitable or unnecessary for use in the little house, but Aunt Bessy had expressed a strong wish to have a number of old-fashioned photo albums at her disposal. Patience remembered them as being plush or leather covered, very heavy and containing photos of distant relations, long dead. For some reason Aunt Bessy had set her heart on examining them again and now seemed the right time to see if she could find them.

It had been a bright morning when she had set out for the village but as she dragged the old-fashioned wooden steps up the stairs she noticed how very dark it was growing. There was no light on the landing and none in the loft; she went back to the kitchen and found a candlestick and a box of matches. There was a distant rumble of thunder as she went upstairs and she cocked an uneasy ear, hoping that the next one would be even more distant. It wasn't; it was a good deal nearer and she lighted her candle with a hand which wasn't quite steady. She was a sensible girl, not easily frightened, but thunderstorms scared her.

She could, of course, go swiftly downstairs again and sit in the comparative comfort of the small sitting-room, but it had been an effort to haul the clumsy steps up to the landing, and, besides, once the aunts were back, it would be harder, for they would be full of good advice and offers of help. Aunt Bessy, despite her age, was quite capable of climbing the steps if she had a mind to. Patience arranged the steps just so and with the candle in one hand pushed the cover away from the square opening to the loft.

It was surprisingly roomy up there; it was also pitch dark. A previous owner had boarded up the floor and being on the small side she had no difficulty in standing upright. The trunks, several old-fashioned leather hat boxes and a bundle of umbrellas and walking sticks almost took up all of the space. She put the candle down carefully on one of the hat boxes and turned her attention to the trunks, swallowing a small scream at a clap of thunder, far too near for her liking.

The trunks weren't locked; she unfastened the first one and heaved back its weighty lid. It had been packed neatly; she turned over several elaborate cloaks and dresses all wrapped in tissue paper and found shoes underneath, old-fashioned slippers with buckles and Louis heels, and a quantity of yellowed note-paper, a parcel of fans and a box of assorted buttons. There was no trace of the photo albums. The next roll of thunder, almost overhead now, caused her to drop the lid with something of a thud before she opened a second trunk.

This time she was lucky; the albums, three of them, were on top of a pile of old curtains. She took them out, closed the trunk and did up the straps once more as the thunder crashed deafeningly just above her head. The quiet once it had grumbled its way to an end was a respite during which, if she were quick enough, she could get down the ladder. The albums were heavy, and she would have to throw them down; if she leaned out as far as possible she would be able to do that without damaging them.

She hung rather precariously over the opening, judging the distance, and froze with fright. Someone had come into the house; the front door was locked but she hadn't closed the back door. Anyone agile enough could climb the fence at the end of the garden; there was a narrow alleyway, overgrown and little used, which ran behind the terrace. She had been a fool; the house had been empty for several weeks and even though she had been going to and fro during the past few days anyone interested would have known by now that she was only there during the day, only it just so happened that she had stayed longer than usual in order to discover the albums.

Mr van der Beek stood in the cramped hall, looking up at her. The sight of her face, white with fright under a fine layer of dust and an old cobweb or two, wrung his heart with tenderness.

He said mildly, 'You shouldn't leave doors open, Patience.'

'Don't you dare speak to me,' she said in a cross voice. 'You frightened the life out of me—you could have been anyone...'

'Exactly, but now you know that it is I, so will you come down?' There was no hint of his strong feelings in his calm voice. 'Why are you up there?'

'I was looking...oh!' She gave a gasp as vivid lightning heralded a crack of thunder. 'I don't like storms,' she told him in a small voice, then, 'Aunt Bessy wanted some photo albums, and it seemed a good chance to look for them.'

He had mounted the narrow stairs and stood inches from her upside-down face. The temptation to reach up and kiss it, cobwebs and all, was great, but he withstood it; time enough for that later.

He said, in the soothing voice he used towards nervous patients, 'Hand them down to me and then come down yourself, but give me that candlestick first before you set the place on fire.'

The face disappeared and a cautious foot took its place, followed by a leg.

'Nice legs,' commented Mr van der Beek.

'Don't you talk to me like that!' The tartness of her voice was swallowed up by reason of another great clap of thunder.

The second foot and leg appeared but before she could get a foothold on the steps he had reached up and lifted her down.

Mr van der Beek, as warm-blooded as the next man despite his remote manner, was possessed of an iron self-control; he let go of her the moment she touched the floor although he allowed himself to dust off a few of the cobwebs and a few feathers from her untidy hair.

'The kitchen?' he asked, picked up the albums and squeezed his bulk against a wall so that she could go downstairs ahead of him. 'I'll just shut the trap, shall I?'

Which gave her a moment to shake the dust out of her clothes. She passed a rather shaky hand over her face too, which was a mistake because it left a smear on one cheek. In the kitchen he offered a snowy handkerchief and she went to the little looking-glass under the clock and took a look. She faced him. 'I'm filthy!' she exclaimed.

He had found a cloth—a clean towel, but he couldn't be expected to know that—and was dusting the albums. The glance he gave her was brief and impersonal. 'No matter—there's no one to see and it makes no difference to me.'

She wiped the worst off, reflecting sadly that of course it made no difference and why should it? Just for a moment she thought a few wicked thoughts about Mevrouw van Teule, the acme of perfection and beauty.

She turned round and saw that he had sat himself on the edge of the kitchen table, looking perfectly at ease.

'I thought you were in Holland. I thought you wouldn't come here ever again. Mr Bennett told me that the house has been sold. It was kind of you to allow us to stay there until I could get this place ready for the aunts. Mrs Dodge is there too; Miss Murch has gone back to your house in Chiswick.' She drew a deep breath. 'So why are you here?'

He didn't answer, only looked at her steadily. She winced and closed her eyes briefly as lightning splashed across the little room. 'It is kind of you...' she began and realised that she had already said that and tried to start again. 'What I mean is, there is no need for the aunts to stay at the house. I'm quite ready here; I only have to pack their things. I thought I'd bring them back tomorrow or the next day.'

'No need. They can stay up at the house...' His stare disconcerted her and she looked away.

'I don't think you quite understand. The new owner will want to move in.' She frowned. 'I must say I do think he might have let me know when he was coming.'

'I'm the new owner,' said Mr van der Beek blandly.

'You're... But you don't want to live here—Miss Murch won't like to come back; she doesn't like the butcher.'

'Miss Murch, bless her, has no need to fret. She will stay at Chiswick and in the course of time will make Dobbs a happy man.'

'Oh, never mind Miss Murch, then,' said Patience, getting cross again. 'Why did you buy the house? You aren't going to live in it, are you?'

'Certainly not; it would be most inconvenient for my work. Your aunts will live there—with Mrs Dodge, of course.'

'But what about me?' She thought she saw then. 'Oh, so that I can be free to find a job and be independent; that would mean they could live on the money from the house quite comfortably.' Then she added, 'Why do you want the aunts to live there? I don't understand...'

'I'm going to be married.'

Her heart dropped into her shoes; she had always laughed at the expression but now she knew that it was true. But there was nothing to do about it but haul it up again with a cheerful face. 'How nice. Mevrouw van Teule told me that you hated to be away from her—I hope—I do hope you'll be very happy.'

Of course he wouldn't be—she couldn't bear the thought of it. A little light-headed, probably because her heart was still in her shoes, she added, 'Of course, she's not the wife for you—you'll be very unhappy...'

She put a grubby hand to her mouth and looked at him in horror. She would have to unsay those words; she was thinking frantically how to do it when he got off the table and came to stand in front of her.

'I should be very unhappy,' he agreed gently, 'but I have—never have had—any intention of marrying Mevrouw van Teule.'

'I still don't understand. Why do you want the house if you're not going to live in it? And why did you buy it?'

He took her hands in his. 'Now listen to me, my darling. Much as I like your aunts, I would not wish to have them live with us, but if they are happy in their old home with someone they know to care for them, could you not see your way to marrying me and living at Rijnsten? And quite often over here in England so that you can visit them whenever you wish.'

'Marry you?' uttered Patience in a wobbly voice.

'Marry me. I find that life is intolerable without you, my dearest love; you are in my mind and my heart and beneath my eyelids when I sleep. I think that I have always loved you.'

Her eyes filled with tears. 'Julius, oh, Julius...' She swallowed the tears and said in a small steady voice, 'I love you too, Julius, but have you considered? I'm—I'm rather plain, you know, and not at all clever. It's very kind of you...'

'Kind, kind?' Mr van der Beek gathered her to his enormous chest. 'My dearest darling, what nonsense is this? Let us have no more of it. You are beautiful and clever and my heart's desire.'

'Really?' asked Patience, and peeped up at him.

'Really.' He kissed her then, gently, but when she smiled up at him his arms tightened around her. 'Presently,' he told her, 'I will tell you just how beautiful and clever you are, but now I am going to kiss you.'

So dreams do come true, thought Patience, and lifted her face to his; she had no idea that being kissed was so very delightful.

Let

HARLEQUIN ROMANCE®

take you

BACK TO THE RANCH

Come to SkyRim Ranch in Bison County, Nebraska!

Meet Abbie Hale, rancher's daughter—a woman who loves her family ranch and loves the ranching life. Then meet Yates Connley, the stranger who comes to SkyRim for Christmas....

Read Bethany Campbell's
The Man Who Came for Christmas,
our next Back to the Ranch title.
Available in December
wherever Harlequin books are sold.

RANCH7

Take 4 bestselling love stories FREE

Plus get a FREE surprise gift!

Special Limited-time Offer

Mail to Harlequin Reader Service®

P. O. Box 609
Fort Erie, Ontario
L2A 5X3

YES! Please send me 4 free Harlequin Romance® novels and my free surprise gift. Then send me 6 brand-new novels every month, which I will receive months before they appear in bookstores. Bill me at the low price of $2.49 each plus 25¢ delivery and GST*. That's the complete price and compared to the cover prices of $2.99 each—quite a bargain! I understand that accepting the books and gift places me under no obligation ever to buy any books. I can always return a shipment and cancel at any time. Even if I never buy another book from Harlequin, the 4 free books and the surprise gift are mine to keep forever.

316 BPA AJJS

Name _____ (PLEASE PRINT)

Address _____ Apt. No. _____

City _____ Province _____ Postal Code _____

This offer is limited to one order per household and not valid to present Harlequin Romance® subscribers
*Terms and prices are subject to change without notice.
Canadian residents will be charged applicable provincial taxes and GST.

CROM-93RR   ©1990 Harlequin Enterprises Limited

Make Christmas a truly Romantic experience—with

HARLEQUIN ROMANCE®

Wouldn't *you* love to kiss a tall, dark Texan under the mistletoe? Gwen does, in HOME FOR CHRISTMAS by Ellen James. Share the experience!

Wouldn't *you* love to kiss a sexy New Englander on a snowy Christmas morning? Angela does, in Shannon Waverly's CHRISTMAS ANGEL. Share the experience!

Look for both of these Christmas Romance titles, available in December wherever Harlequin Books are sold.

(And don't forget that Romance novels make great gifts! Easy to buy, easy to wrap and just the right size for a stocking stuffer. *And* they make a wonderful treat when you need a break from Christmas shopping, Christmas wrapping and stuffing stockings!)

1993 Keepsake

CHRISTMAS

Stories

Capture the spirit and romance of Christmas with KEEPSAKE CHRISTMAS STORIES, a collection of three stories by favorite historical authors. The perfect Christmas gift!

Don't miss these heartwarming stories, available in November wherever Harlequin books are sold:

ONCE UPON A CHRISTMAS by Curtiss Ann Matlock
A FAIRYTALE SEASON by Marianne Willman
TIDINGS OF JOY by Victoria Pade

ADD A TOUCH OF ROMANCE TO YOUR HOLIDAY SEASON WITH KEEPSAKE CHRISTMAS STORIES!

HX93

When the only time you have for yourself is...

Christmas is such a busy time—with shopping, decorating, writing cards, trimming trees, wrapping gifts....

When you do have a few *stolen moments* to call your own, treat yourself to a brand-new *short* novel. Relax with one of our Stocking Stuffers— or with all six!

Each STOLEN MOMENTS title is a complete and original contemporary romance that's the perfect length for the busy woman of the nineties! Especially at Christmas...

And they make perfect **stocking stuffers**, too! (For your mother, grandmother, daughters, friends, co-workers, neighbors, aunts, cousins—all the other women in your life!)

Look for the STOLEN MOMENTS display in December

STOCKING STUFFERS:

HIS MISTRESS Carrie Alexander
DANIEL'S DECEPTION Marie DeWitt
SNOW ANGEL Isolde Evans
THE FAMILY MAN Danielle Kelly
THE LONE WOLF Ellen Rogers
MONTANA CHRISTMAS Lynn Russell

HSM2

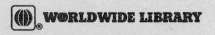 **WORLDWIDE LIBRARY**